Trouble at the Mill

A Case for Crabbe and Crabbe

Geoffrey Foster

March 2011

Geoffrey Foster was born in London, England in 1933, and his childhood was mostly spent in Kent, in southeast England, where there are towns like Woodhampton.

His father was a London policeman most of his working life, and his mother, when she worked, was a shorthand typist (a stenographer). He has two sisters, five and thirteen years younger than himself.

He went to public elementary and secondary schools and then to the University of Cambridge, where he studied engineering. Moving to Australia in 1959, he taught Mechanical Engineering at the University of Queensland for 14 years, before switching to educational development. He took early retirement in 1995.

As well as writing, he likes reading, listening to music, solving cryptic crosswords, walking the family beagle, Kafka, and playing tennis with his younger sister, Ynes.

Also by Geoffrey Foster:

Kit and the Beeman	ISBN 978-0-9805310-0-8
Kit the Venturer	ISBN 978-0-9805310-1-5
Vincent the Beeman	ISBN 978-0-9805310-2-2
Beatrice's Birthday	ISBN 978-0-9805310-3-9
Beatrice and Vincent's Welsh Adventures	
	ISBN 978-0-9805310-4-6

This volume:	ISBN 978-0-9805310-6-0

Chapter 1

"Well, we're nearly there, Alex – I'll take the wheel now, if you can bear to let go of it!" The speaker was Melpomene Crabbe, née Musgrave, and she was addressing her bridegroom Alexander, who was indeed clinging to the wheel of the red Alvis two-seat roadster that he had been happily driving for the past hour.

Melpomene, a slight figure of medium height, muffled up in a long dust-coat and scarf, with a soft-peaked cap set backwards on her head, vaulted nimbly over the passenger door as they pulled up and then walked round to the driver's side, while Alex, similarly dressed, stood up and changed seats.

Soon they were humming along a country road, between hedges, until Melpomene spotted a sign-post saying "Private Road: Woodhampton Castle Hotel Only." She took the turn a little too fast for the dusty surface, so she had to control an incipient fish-tail, and then drove more carefully down the drive until the impressive porte-cochère of the hotel could be seen.

As the car drew up, a servant came out to open the driver's door and hand Melpomene down, while Alex showed a second man to where the cases were strapped to a rack on the back of the Alvis. A dignified grey-haired gentleman then descended the steps with the aid of a walking-stick and took Melpomene's hands, saying, "Welcome back, Miss Melpomene – or should I say Madam? It seems a long time since you last visited us."

"Well we have been rather busy in Town, setting up our practice, you know, but we're certainly very happy to see you again, Mr Grimshaw. Are the rest of the staff all the same as before?" "Oh yes, Miss Melpomene, including those few who used to be your parents' staff before the castle was turned into a hotel – no doubt you will meet them all later. We have prepared the best suite for you and your husband. I imagine you would like to have a bath and change before dinner? You may recognize some of the other guests – we shall see!"

Feeling fresh and rested after their baths, they changed into their evening clothes. Melpomene chose a rather restrained dress, a compromise between the flapper and the correct in style, not knowing who else would be at dinner, but livened it up with a string of pearls that hung low down her bare back. Alex, of course, wore an ordinary dinner jacket.

As they entered the dining room, they were greeted by several people, including Melpomene's mother, Lady Cynthia, and two of her aunts, who beckoned them to sit with them, Melpomene next to her Mama, and Alex opposite, next to a gentlemen who was introduced as Major Buckmaster. A long series of conversations ensued, mainly of the trivial, "Where did you spend the winter?" kind. It was not until they had enjoyed an excellent soup and a delicious entrée, that the conversation became slightly more serious.

Lady Cynthia was the first to broach the subject of her daughter's new occupation, "I hear that you and Alex have set yourselves up like Sherlock Holmes, dear, I do hope that you have not sunk to recovering lost cats or accusing ladies' maids of pilfering their mistresses' pearls! Will you tell me what you are really doing?"

Melpomene saw that Major Buckmaster, and even the aunts, had little idea of what her Mama was referring to, so decided to present them with some sort of cohesive story.

"I should explain things from the beginning." she said, "It started when we met each other as students in London. Alex was in the last term of his law degree, at University College, and I had just done my final examinations in social anthropology at the LSE."

"Whatever is that?" asked Aunt Isabel, who was a little older than her sister Cynthia, and as far as Melpomene knew, was involved only in charitable activities and bridge.

"Do you mean 'LSE' or 'social anthropology'?" asked Melpomene, smiling brightly to indicate she was not being unkind. "One is the London School of Economics, and the other is, broadly, the study of how people relate and communicate, even those who are blind, or have a hearing impairment."

Aunt Isabel looked suitably impressed, and decided not to ask any more questions. Melpomene continued, "Well, to cut a long story short, Alex and I fell in love, and then, after many long discussions, we decided that since neither of us wanted to continue in the academic life, Alex could become a sort of solicitor, but with extras, and I could join him as an expert partner. So we set up as a detective agency. And, so far, it has proved quite successful. We haven't tracked down any lost pets, nor caught any ladies' maids with their hands in jewel cases, but we have managed to solve one or two quite serious crimes. But this is hardly dinner-table conversation, so perhaps we could turn to matters more pleasant!"

Major Buckmaster, who had been wriggling a little in his seat, said, "Of course we should certainly stop talking shop, as it were, but before we do, I would like to declare my interest. I am the principal magistrate in Woodhampton, and I am also a great friend of Superintendent Wilkinson of the local constabulary. Perhaps we could catch up on matters forensic on a later occasion!"

The rest of the meal, over dessert, cheese and fruit, was spent on accounts of local social events, the prowess of various young relatives and similar undemanding topics. When the end of dinner was called, Lady Cynthia explained that, here in the country, it was not the custom for the men to go and smoke and enjoy port separately, while their wives were left to talk about flower-arranging, but that all the guests would proceed to a drawing room where they could talk to whomever they pleased, about whatever they wished. And there would be card tables there for those who wanted a few rubbers of bridge, or even some hands of the new South American game, Canasta.

And, rather surprisingly, it turned out that Major Buckmaster played the piano well, and entertained whoever wanted to listen with a selection of classical pieces, interspersed with coarse music-hall songs, in which he was joined enthusiastically by some otherwise respectable-seeming ladies.

All considering, the evening passed very pleasantly, and Melpomene and Alex, seeing the hour was advancing, excused themselves, saying that the car journey had relaxed them to the point that they were ready for bed. There were kisses all round from Lady Cynthia and the aunts, and from one or two other ladies who had been playing cards with them.

As they climbed the stairs to their suite, Alex remarked that he had been apprehensive about coming, but that now he was entirely relaxed and even turning his mind towards activities such as golf or, better still, long walks in the countryside.

"And there are tennis-courts here, you know!" said Melpomene. "Don't think you will avoid healthy exercise – golf is simply a good walk ruined, if you ask me!"

Chapter 2

The next morning promised to develop into one of those delightful days of early Autumn, with a bright sky and a slight nip in the air – just right for tennis, as Melpomene announced. So, after a hearty breakfast of kedgeree, eggs and bacon and marmalade toast, she and Alex headed for the courts. In the pavilion they found a selection of racquets for those, like themselves, who had not brought their own, and took a dozen balls from the huge chest there, picking out those that were whitest and still had most of their nap.

There were three courts, one of them already occupied by doubles players, comprising the versatile Major Buckmaster, partnering a young girl of about fourteen, who could have been his daughter, and their opponents, a couple in their thirties perhaps, who appeared to be undergoing a sound thrashing.

As Melpomene and Alex took their court and started to warm up, the Major, trying to reach a wide ball, slipped and fell. "I'm all right!" he called hastily, "but I've picked up a huge grass stain on the knee of my flannels – they'll have to go to the dry-cleaners in town, I expect. Never mind, play on, Phoebe!"

Once they had got the feel of things, the couple enjoyed an increasingly vigorous succession of games, and after an hour, with honours fairly even, they decided that enough was enough for one morning. In the pavilion, where there were jugs of lemonade on beds of ice and bath buns set out, the Major and his friends were apparently having a post-mortem on their play.

In fact, their opponents were having a rather testy argument, and as Melpomene and Alex came in, the wife was saying, "Well, that's it, Norman – if you are going to keep on giving me smart bits of advice all through the game, you can go and coach your little friend from the office instead, in future!"

Then Buckmaster, trying to be placatory, said, "Now then, Melinda, you two were not playing badly, it's just that Phoebe and I have been partners for ages, so that we work together very well!"

To that, Melinda burst into tears, shook her husband's hand off her shoulder, and rushed out of the pavilion. Norman shrugged and made an apologetic face at the others and followed her, but not particularly fast.

Later on, back in the foyer of the hotel, they found Major Buckmaster talking to the housekeeper, Mrs Arkwright, who was saying, "No need to bother with the dry-cleaners, Major, leave your flannels with the chambermaid and we will get them looking like new by tomorrow – I presume you have others with you? Let us see, you're booked in with us until Monday, is that right?"

"Oh, thank you, Mrs Arkwright, dependable as usual! Yes, I have to be on the bench on Tuesday. My wife will pick Phoebe and me up after dinner on Monday – we don't want to miss another Woodhampton Castle meal!"

Seeing Melpomene and Alex, the Major said, "An enjoyable game? Sorry about the unpleasantness in the pavilion, I'm afraid that Mr and Mrs Felton are going through a bit of a patch at the moment, in fact I believe they came here this weekend in an attempt at reconciliation – which appears not to be working too well! But enough idle gossip, I would really like to talk to you two about your detective practice, whenever you have some time and feel like it."

"No time like the present," said Alex, "OK with you dear? We could find a nice quiet place and maybe chat over a before-lunch drink."

When they were settled comfortably on cane chairs in the garden room, with a bottle or two of chilled white wine, Buckmaster started his questioning. "By the bye," he said, "call me Stephen, you can't keep on saying Major all the time, and I will use your first names as well if I may. I would like you to tell me all about your set-up, eventually, but first I would like to hear your reactions to a case that's recently come up here – would that be all right?"

"Of course!" said Melpomene, "And after a while you can even start calling me Mel – but not Pom, please, that's reserved for my little brother's use! So tell us about your case."

"To start with, it might surprise you to know that not far out of Woodhampton, about a dozen miles to the West, there is a flourishing woolen mill. There are many in Wiltshire and Somerset, but they are unusual in this area. And I think that this is part of the problem, because many of the skilled mill-

5

hands have been enticed away from their familiar surroundings and even their families. Anyway, this all began when I had a weaver brought up before me one Monday morning on a D and D – that's a drunk and disorderly charge, you know. I get a lot of these on Monday mornings, you might guess why! Thankfully, the court is shut next Monday for the Bank Holiday – but Bank Holiday celebrations will probably produce another crop for Tuesday!"

"At first this seemed an ordinary case, a PC gave evidence that the accused had been in a brawl outside a pub and I was all set to levy the normal fine and warning and send him on his way, when he put up his hand, like a kid in class, and said, 'Excuse me, your worship, can I ast you summat? Why weren't the other one picked up – I were on'y trying to get the gun off 'im?' At this, I asked the police officer, who was still in the stand, what this was all about. The PC had the grace to blush and said that he knew nothing of any gun, whereupon a woman in the visitors' gallery shouted, 'Well, you was the on'y one there what didn't – that bloke was a-wavin' of it around in front of everyone in the public!' Consternation all round, so I called for an adjournment and had the original accused sent back to the holding cells!"

"I had the PC come to my rooms and called for the Station Sergeant, but I got no further with them, so I sent my clerk to the pub to make enquiries of the landlord and the barman who was on that night. Strangely, no one knew anything further, so I'm at a loss. There is a plain-clothes CID officer at the station and he tried to make discreet enquiries, but came up with nothing more, so I had to let the accused go after he had paid his fine. By that time he had spent four nights in the lock-up, so I thought that was enough for the poor fellow. Now, what would a real detective have done in these circumstances?"

Melpomene asked, "When did all this happen? Maybe the trail has gone cold by now." "Well, it was only early this week – the CID man was there on Wednesday." Melpomene continued, "Was there any attempt made to list those in the bar at the relevant time?"

The Major looked a little put out, "Well, of course, we may be from the provinces, but we do know a thing or two about proper investigative procedures. My clerk has a list that he was given and DC Miller, the CID man, added a few more names to it. I have the list in my office safe at the courthouse."

Chapter 3

Said Melpomene, "Would you trust me with a copy of that list, Stephen? And tell me which pub it was – there used to be three of them here altogether, were there not?"

"Certainly you shall have a copy, er, Mel – the pub concerned was the Green Man, opposite St Matthew's, do you remember it? The inn-keeper is a decent man, Jim Webster, but the public bar attracts a very mixed patronage, mostly farm-workers, but with some hands from the woolen mill. There's a regular bus that runs between the mill and the town, and a lot of the single workers come in for a drink and to play skittles in the evenings, there's no pub any nearer the works. Are you intending to ask more questions there?"

"Not for the moment, Stephen. I'll go there on Monday, I think and simply look and listen. Since it's a bank holiday then, there will probably be a lot of regular customers there in the afternoon and evening, what do you think?"

"Very likely, Mel, but be careful, there are not a lot of respectable young women who go to the public bar at the Green Man very much, so you might get chatted up!"

"I think I can cope with that, but maybe I'll take a minder with me, eh, Alex? But I won't let on I know him, it might be handy for us to work independently some of the time. We'll see! Now, Stephen, enough of work discussions for today! Since it's Sunday tomorrow, do you and your daughter have any religious objections to playing tennis on the Sabbath? If Alex is up for it, we should like to challenge you to a doubles match in the morning!"

"That sounds delightful, Mel – I'm sure that Phoebe will be keen, too! We're going to the pictures this evening, – they're showing 'The Thief of Bagdad', with Douglas Fairbanks and Anna May Wong, at the Palace – I've heard that it's worth seeing! Do you feel like coming, too?"

"No, thank you very much for asking, Stephen, but Alex and I saw it last week in the West End. We can thoroughly recommend it, can't we darling?"

The dining room was not as full this night, but Melpomene's Mama and her aunts were still there and invited Melpomene and Alex to sit with them. On an adjacent table were the couple from the tennis-courts, the Feltons – not arguing this time, but rather sitting and picking at their plates in a stony silence. The dinner was largely salads and other cold dishes, but was nevertheless delicious.

At the end of the meal, Lady Cynthia said, "Will you come to the sitting room for bridge? I do not play myself, as I am somewhat scatter-brained, I fear, but there are usually some keen players to be found. As they entered there were already three tables in play, and Mr and Mrs Felton were standing looking undecided. Taking the bull by the horns, Alex approached them, saying, "Would you make up a table with us? We do not claim to be expert players, but we can probably give you a decent game – I am Alex and this is my wife, Melpomene."

Mr Felton's face brightened, "Didn't we see you on the court this morning? May I present my wife, Melinda? I am Norman. Melinda is called Mel by her friends." "So am I!" exclaimed Melpomene, "perhaps we would be safer to stick with our full names to avoid confusion!" They all laughed, and this seemed to relax the Feltons somewhat.

The first few hands were straightforward enough, and honours were about even, but during the bidding for the next hand, Melinda started looking annoyed and then burst out, "There is no point muttering under your breath, Norman! If you don't like my bids we had better call the whole thing off!" She threw her cards on the table and stormed off. Mr Felton stood, looking very embarrassed, apologized and followed her out of the room.

"There is something strange going on there!" said Melpomene, "Do you recall Melinda's remark this morning about Norman's 'little friend'? Methinks there is a story here!"

Lady Cynthia came over, saying, "Oh dear, it's always upsetting when people quarrel in public, is it not? We haven't known the Feltons long, he is the new works manager at Gormsby's, the woollen mill, you know. I must admit I'm rather intrigued!"

After a sound night's sleep, Melpomene and Alex woke to another perfect Autumn day. Stephen Buckmaster and Phoebe were at breakfast, already in their tennis clothes, as were Mel and Alex. Stephen's flannels showed no sign of grass stains, and the girls were dressed almost identically, in sleeveless white dresses with dropped waists – 'very flapper', as Alex remarked.

They played two energetic sets of doubles and by the end were quite happy to stop and relax over the cool drinks and snacks in the pavilion. Stephen and his daughter won both sets, but by modest margins.

"How was the picture?" Melpomene asked Phoebe, "Did you swoon over Douglas Fairbanks?" Phoebe laughed, saying, "I think he would prefer more exotic and experienced women than I – but it was a good movie, Father and I both enjoyed it very much. You must meet my mother later – she will be bringing my little brother to the hotel this afternoon. She had to stay at home this weekend, because Grandmama is living with us for a while, and she is rather frail. This afternoon a good friend will be sitting with her."

They all sat together for lunch, but while they were at the fruit salad, a hotel servant came over and called Stephen to the phone. When he returned, he said, "I'm afraid you will have to excuse me, the police are sending a car to pick me up and take me to the mill – there has been some sort of happening there which requires my attention, I can't think what, the officer on the phone was being very cagey."

As promised, Phoebe introduced Mel and Alex to her Mama, Eugenie, and her little brother Marcus, a cherubic three-year-old with an evil grin. "He's quite a handful!" said Phoebe, as she grabbed him before he could run into the garden.

They agreed that, all the same, he had the right idea, so they strolled together through the gardens, while Phoebe kept a firm hold of Marcus' arm. "What we need is a dog lead!" she exclaimed in some frustration.

After an hour or so, it felt like time to go onto the terrace, where tea was being served, so they quietened Marcus with a huge currant bun, and took their seats where they could survey the extensive grounds.

"I wonder where Stephen has got to?" said Eugenie after a while. "I do hope this is not going to spoil the entire long week-end."

And, as if in response, there was Major Buckmaster, rather red in the face, hurrying towards them.

Chapter 4

Stephen sat down heavily, and rather breathlessly gestured toward the teacups. Phoebe took the hint and fetched him a cup, which he downed thirstily. "Thank you, my dear, I needed that! What it is to be a slave of the public – or of the police force, more's the point! Do you know why I was fetched? Simply because Superintendent Wilkinson – really a very decent fellow, but a bit hide-bound – did not want to take responsibility for what he feared might be seen as destruction of private property! I'll have a second cup – more sugar this time, please Phoebe – and then I'll relate this properly."

"Well," he went on, "it all started with a call from the caretaker of Gormsby Mill, who lives in a little flat over the factory main gate, to the police-station here, to report intruders. He had been sitting by his front window having a smoke when he heard a noise – in the main weaving-shed, he thought, He said to the policeman when he arrived that it had sounded to him like heavy equipment being knocked over. He grabbed his bunch of keys, went down the stairs and tried to open the big doors to the shed where all the looms are, but found that they wouldn't open – apparently they were jammed from the inside."

"He called out 'anyone there?' but of course there was no answer, so he started cautiously walking round the shed, on the outside, peering into some of the windows as he went. As I saw, when he took me and Wilkinson round later, the windows are all barred, and most of them are painted over – either for privacy or so that the workers won't be distracted by outside views, I suppose, so he couldn't see much."

"At the far end of the shed, which is maybe a couple of hundred yards long, there are some outside iron stairs which lead up to a first-floor office area. His keys worked this time, so he went in and through a main drawing office to where there are windows giving a view across the top of the looms and other machinery. And from there he could see movement halfway along the shed, two or three people seemed to be doing something, he couldn't see what. He went back out of the office area, down the steps and met Superintendent Wilkinson and two policemen who had arrived and were looking around. Together they tried the large doors at that end of the shed, but they had been jammed as well."

"Well, to cut a long story short, eventually I was summoned to the scene. Wilkinson explained that he wanted to get in somehow, by breaking down the doors if necessary, but when he had said this to the caretaker, Arthur Watson, he was told that the proprietors of the works would not like this one little bit. That was when he decided to phone me and shift the responsibility onto my shoulders, dear fellow! I had no hesitation in giving him the go-ahead. As you would well know as a lawyer, young Alex, the police have a special status in this country and it was well within their powers to do any amount of breaking in if they had reasons to suspect criminal activity."

Melpomene was getting quite fidgety and excited by this time, and said, "But you are deliberately saving the good bits up, Stephen, and keeping us on tenterhooks – aren't you ever going to disclose to us the nature of this criminal activity? Or must we wait to read about it in the newspapers?"

"Patience, my dear, patience! I shall get there! Arthur the caretaker took us round the end of the weaving shed, and we could see another building, of much the same size, that he told us they called the warehouse. There is a railway siding running into it from the end where we were, with a couple of closed wagons waiting ready to be loaded. But the most important thing was that there was a toolshed. Arthur opened it up and the two PCs armed themselves with a large crowbar apiece. Within the space of five minutes or less, we were pushing open the great doors of the weaving shed and venturing in. We had not been able to avoid making a noise, and the next thing we saw was three figures making rapidly for the doors at the far end, the first ones the caretaker had tried. Our two policemen gave pursuit, still carrying their crowbars and blowing their whistles – more out of habit rather than to any purpose, I thought."

"The fugitives reached the doors and started to take away the baulks of timber they had propped up against them, but they were not fast enough and one of the policemen shouted 'No use lads, you might as well give up, there are more of us coming!' The malefactors swung round, and Wilkinson and I – we had arrived at the scene by then – could see for the first time that what we had was a man and two young boys, maybe twelve or thirteen years old."

"And to my surprise I recognized the man – he was my D and D from last week! We didn't try to question them on the spot – I suggested that this would better done at the station, where their statements could be taken down properly. So I left them ringing up for a paddy-wagon and got the police driver to bring me back here. So, Melpomene, I must leave you in some suspense – I can tell you no more than that as yet! Perhaps you will pick up some more of the background to this mystery when you visit the pub tomorrow."

While Stephen tucked into a plate of sandwiches that Eugenie had ordered for him, the rest of the group started speculating about the activities of the miscreants.

"I can't believe that it was a robbery," said Alex, "what could they hope to get from a weaving shed that would be valuable and portable enough to be worth taking?"

"How about sabotage?" suggested Eugenie, "Maybe someone has a grudge against the mill and wanted to put some of the looms out of action."

Melpomene had a more romantic idea, "Stephen's poor D and D is suffering from such ennui that he is frantically seeking for excitement, by picking fights or leading his young devotees astray! Next he will steal a car, maybe, or do something outrageous in the town square!"

Stephen grunted at this, "In my judgment, I would doubt that this man has the intelligence or imagination for any of these – my guess, and it is only a guess – is that he is working for someone who put him up to it. We might find out more later when Melpomene investigates further. By the way, my dear, have you had any further thoughts about how you intend to go about it?"

"What I will rely on, Stephen, are my skills in analysis that I have developed from my studies in social anthropology. The whole discipline is based on the notion that people behave in terms of the system of relationships within which each of us works and lives. Let me, as a rough-and-ready example, point to our acquaintances, Mr and Mrs Felton. All of us here, with the possible exception of Marcus, have picked up sufficient knowledge of society to see that this couple has a problem which each of them is dealing with in contrasting ways. So, when I go to the pub, I will be trying to see whether there are any social relationships of interest among those who regularly frequent the public bar. End of lecture – any questions?"

Chapter 5

On Monday morning, Melpomene and Alex put their heads together, to plan their visit to 'The Green Man' and to marshal the information they had picked up so far, which wasn't much. "All we know really," remarked Melpomene, "is that there is something fishy going on at Gormsby Mill, and that our famed D and D champion is involved in some way – has Stephen mentioned his name at all?" "Yes," said Alex, "he is called Will Brooks, Stephen said, he thinks he only came here when the mill opened up."

"In a sense," said Melpomene, "it's a pity they have put him away again – it would have been valuable to find out by direct observation who his associates, or even his rivals or enemies, might be. I shall have to work from a clean slate, as it were, and see what, if anything, I can deduce about the social structures in the public bar of the Green Man as of today's date. If this were an academic exercise, I would take notes openly, but I don't want to draw attention to what I'm doing here – the local population is probably already wary of strangers like us."

"I have an idea!" said Alex, "how about taking a copy of The Times in with you – you can settle yourself in a corner with a drink and maybe a snack and pretend to tackle the crossword – and then you can make your notes in the margin and people will think you are working out anagrams or something, if they bother at all! Meanwhile I can see if the vapid conversation of a visiting townee can bring us any tit-bits."

"Excellent, my darling! In any case, I always gaze around blankly when I'm doing the crossword – and when this case is all over I shall write a methodology article for one of the anthropology journals!"

They drove into town in the Alvis at about 11.30, and while Alex was parking it in the street outside the pub, Melpomene was walking there from a couple of streets away. As she entered the public bar, she could see that Alex was already drinking beer and chatting with a couple of the more elderly locals, but she didn't even glance at him. She went to the bar, asked the landlord whether they were doing ploughman's lunches yet, ordered a cider and found a nice place on a seat in a bay window, which gave her a good view of the whole room.

In a few minutes the lunch – a crusty roll, a slab of butter, a great wodge of cheddar cheese and several pickled onions – was brought to her, and while she was starting on it she unfolded the newspaper and turned to the crossword. To establish what she was doing, she tut-tutted as she was rummaging in her handbag, and then went over to the bar and asked in a fairly loud voice whether she could borrow a pencil. The landlord produced a rather chewed-down stump, but then sharpened it for her with a pocket-knife. "Thanks!" she said, "I don't feel right until I've done my daily crossword!"

A man who was sitting at the bar commented, "Just like me, missus, till I've had me daily pint!" to which the landlord chipped in, "And the rest, Jemmy, and the rest!"

As she went back to her place in the window, Melpomene saw that three men sitting at a table on the way seemed to have been discussing what was written on a sheet of paper, and she was interested to note that one of them covered it up with his hand as she sidled past, the tables being quite closely spaced. They returned to their task and their chatting once she was sitting down again. So Melpomene's first note on the newspaper was, "3 w/paper; cagey; poss. millworkers – not farm boots: Sam, Vince, third no name said."

In between filling in squares, she kept her ears open and was soon aware of what sounded like the telling of long tale by a little man with white whiskers, "I tell 'ee, before the mill come we had none of them ruckuses of a Sat'dy night – we sometimes got turned out before closing when we was singing too 'earty, but that was all. Now, you can bet on some sort of a fight every time – either one of us locals picks on a weaver, or the other way about. But never so bad as last week! I never saw no-one threatened wi' a shotgun before! O'course, it were stupid of Paddy to bring his gun in with 'im, even if it were stowed in 'is poacher's pocket – did you see the bird he handed over to Jim Webster? That'd be good for a few rounds o' drinks, I reckon."

"So, Lenny, what was he and Brooksy arguing about then?" asked one of his three companions. Lenny laughed, "What else but a woman, o'course! Anyone can see they're both sweet on Elsie Pickford, her what works as a loom-setter over at Gormsby's! She's stringing 'em along all right – prob'ly got another couple on the go, too, saucy wench!"

Melpomene made further notes, and then went to the bar for another cider. "You sure, Miss?" said Jim, "Our local cider is most likely stronger than what you're used to in London!"

"How did you know I'm from London?" she asked. "Ah well, some of the hotel staff are reg'lars here, Miss, and they 'aven't taken no vow o' silence, them, 'ave they!"

Melpomene made another note, mental this time, that Jim Webster would be a valuable source of information, but that they should catch him some time when he was away from the bar. She carried her cider back to her place and finished her lunch while she was sipping it. She turned her attention to two young men who had just come in and were collecting sets of darts and tankards of beer from Jim, and lining up in front of the dartboard. "Two hundred and one up suit you, Mike?" said the first, a tall man with red hair who looked more like a clerk than a worker, and his friend, likewise probably an office-worker, replied, "OK, Brian, shall we make it half-a-crown to start with?"

They played seriously, with very little banter, so Melpomene looked elsewhere, until she heard the red-head say, in between games, "Did you take Elsie to the pictures on Saturday, like you said? How was it?" "Well the picture was great, Brian, I could really go for Anna May Wong, chink or not, but I got nowhere with Miss Pickford – Elsie I mean, not Mary!" They both laughed.

Melpomene wondered whether the sociable Elsie Pickford might also be worth interviewing on her own, with the careful adoption of a certain amount of finesse. Maybe Alex could exert some of his charm on her?

There seemed to be an end to the collection of useful information and, to decide things definitely, a charabanc-load of trippers arrived and streamed into the pub, the men preferring the public, while their female companions opted for the snug.

Melopomene, rose, thanked the landlord nicely as she returned his pencil, and went out. She inclined her head as she passed Alex, indicating which way she would walk, and a few minutes and a couple of streets later, he drew up and she hopped into the Alvis. "Take plenty of notes, dear?" he asked, "I must write mine up as soon as we can. Being a lawyer is good practice!"

Chapter 6

They got back to the hotel in time for afternoon tea, and Melpomene was happy to see that it was a Devonshire cream affair this time, with scones, strawberry jam and clotted cream. Even after her ploughman's lunch, which would have given any ploughman enough energy for a full day's work, she pitched into it with zest, washing the scones down with two cups of Lapsang Souchong tea, one of her favourites. While she was so engaged, with Alex taking a less enthusiastic approach, Norman Felton approached, on his own, asking whether he might join them, saying, quite unnecessarily, "Melinda has a headache, so she is resting until dinner."

"I'm glad to see you, Norman, please sit down, these scones are scrumptious," said Melpomene, "maybe this is a good time to ask you a couple of technical questions about the mill. I have picked up some bits and pieces of information, but this leaves me with a couple of gaps and I'm a naturally inquisitive person. Would that be all right?"

"Fire away!" said Felton, "I'm at your disposal."

"Well, first, I have always got the impression, from novels and stories set in a weaving context, that weavers are usually women – am I right?" "Well, that would indeed be the case for the Lancashire cotton trades, and even for Yorkshire woolens, but what we have, here and in the West Country, is a different industry, dealing with heavier fabrics, such as blankets and tweeds – which, by the way, are now mostly factory-made, instead of being woven by hand in cottages on the Scottish Isles – and even with carpets. This calls for heavier looms and therefore for male weavers. Most of the Gormsby weavers are in fact men."

"But you do employ some women, I gather."

"Oh yes, Melpomene, we do have a few women weavers – hefty ladies they are, too – and most of our loom-setters are girls, which is normal in this industry. They have a more precise touch than men, which is what is needed in setting up a loom – if the set-up is not completely exact, the cloth comes out very uneven. If you like, I'll arrange a visit for you, and you can see all this, if as you say, you are interested."

"Oh, that would be lovely!" said Melpomene, "Can Alex come too?" "Of course he can, no problem! How about tomorrow morning, about 9 – we start work at 8, but after the holiday break there are bound to be one or two hitches. Ask at the gate to be directed to my office."

So the next morning, at the appointed time, Melpomene drove the Alvis in through the factory gates and spoke to the man who came out of the gate-house to greet them, saying they had come to see Mr Felton.

"You can park up there beside the shed," he told them, "that black Daimler is his car. If you go up those iron stairs, anyone inside will direct you to his office." He saluted, and they drove off.

Opening the door at the top of the stairs they were greeted by the din of the machines, which Alex thought sounded like a million typewriters clicking away. Inside the offices it was a little quieter, and when they were shown into Norman Felton's office it was even more subdued. He was talking to a young woman holding a pile of papers, and waved to Melpomene and Alex to come in and sit down.

The woman left, saying, "You won't forget to go and see about the mix-up in aisle 12, will you, Mr Felton?" He reassured her and then turned to his visitors, saying with a wry smile, "As it happens we've been given an opportunity to see an example of the perpetual conflict between the loom-setters and the weavers! I'll explain more when we're down there. I'll lend you some ear-muffs – I'm used to the noise of the looms, but you might find it painful!"

He led them down some internal stairs to the main floor of the shed. Melpomene was grateful for the ear-muffs – the noise would have been overpowering without them. There was row after row of looms, all driven by belts from overhead shafting, with leather belts flapping as they drove the looms.

Norman Felton spoke loudly but Melpomene had to lift the muffs a little to hear what he was saying, "Each weaver has five or six looms to work – his main task is to watch them and to look out for breaks in the thread, which happen quite often, have a look here, conveniently for us it's happening as we watch."

The weaver threw a lever, which moved the driving belt aside, and as soon as the loom stopped, he knotted the thread, checked it and set his loom going again.

Norman went on, "You can see that it is very trying work, and weavers tend to have very short tempers as a result. Follow me, I have to attend to some sort of difficulty in aisle 12."

He led the way past several rows of looms till they came to an aisle where some sort of altercation was going on beside a loom that was stopped. A weaver, red in the face, was gesticulating at a young woman in a whitish overall, shouting things like "How can a man do his work proper if 'is loom ain't set up right? There's heddles missing here, what the 'eck are you up to?"

Felton tapped him on the shoulder, and led him and the girl to a door at the side of the shed, followed by Melpomene and Alex. Closing the door behind them, it was apparent they were in a corridor leading to washrooms and lavatories – it was a lot quieter here.

"Tell me what this is all about," Norman asked the pair. "Like I said, me loom is not set up right. There's s'posed to be 650 warp threads on this run, so 650 heddles – but there's no more than 600 as you can easily see!"

The girl, close to tears, said, "I set this up proper on Friday night, along with the others in this aisle, before we went off shift. There was 650 threads and heddles then all right – see me paper!" She gave Felton a board with half-a-dozen sheets clipped to it, which he took and looked at carefully.

"So are you saying," he asked her, "that someone has been interfering with the loom between then and now?"

"Either that or she's telling us lies!" interjected the weaver, "The others in me row are all right, it's only that one that's set up bad!"

"Well," said Felton, "we can't waste any more production time now. What are your names? Steve Briggs and Elsie Pickford?" He made a note. "OK, Briggs, go back and run your other looms – I hope nothing broke while we were here talking. And Elsie, take your charts and go and set up that loom from scratch – you must have plenty of spare heddles, is that right?" "Oh, yes, Sir, thank you Sir!" said Elsie, actually curtseying before she went back into the shed.

Chapter 7

Back in Norman Felton's office, he forestalled their obvious questions, saying, "Yes, I have a lot of instructing to do – but first, can I offer you a cup of tea and a biscuit?" He rang a little bell on his desk, and the clerk who they had seen before appeared. "Three teas and some biscuits, please, Maureen. Do you both take milk and sugar? Never mind, dear, why don't you bring both?"

"Now let me show you something you have been wondering about, I'll wager!" He opened his desk drawer and produced a small object, a shiny strip of metal a few inches long, with a loop at each end and an eye in the centre. "This is a heddle!" he announced proudly, "each of the warp threads is passed through this eye in the middle, so that the heddles can be used to move the warp up or down, to form the 'shed' that the shuttle is shot through for every row of the weft."

Melpomene and Alex still looked rather blank, so he went on to give them a short lesson in weaving, until they both started nodding their heads in comprehension, and then he added, "When we've finished here, have a good look at a loom working on the way out, and it will all become clear, I'm sure!"

They finished their tea, thanked Norman profusely, and then took their leave, taking a short turn round the nearest aisle of looms before they left.

Back in the car, Alex driving this time, Melpomene said, with some satisfaction, "Well, apart from our lesson in weaving technology, we have learned three very important facts this morning. First, we now have a very good idea what Brooks and his juvenile assistants were doing on Sunday when they were surprised by Stephen Buckmaster and the police – removing heddles and ruining the loom set-up. If they hadn't been disturbed they might have got to many more looms than the one we have just found out about."

"So this was indeed sabotage," said Alex, "and we next need to find out on whose behalf it was done – a business rival, perhaps. What are the other two things you picked up?"

"They both concern Norman Felton's love-life! One negative and one positive," declared Melpomene. "First of all, whatever shenanigans dear Elsie Pickford may be getting up to, having an affair with the boss is not one of them! I was observing both of them carefully, and there was not a shred of evidence of a relationship to be seen! No, I think that Norman's 'little friend from the office', who Melinda Felton mentioned in the tennis pavilion is clearly Maureen!"

"But," said Alex, "I saw no evidence of anything between them either! Perhaps I'm looking for the wrong indications, am I? I sometimes feel I'm working at a disadvantage compared with you, my dear."

"No, don't berate yourself, Alex, I wouldn't love you as I do if you were stupid! It's simply because you're a solicitor, not a social anthropologist! Didn't you notice that Maureen hardly ever looked directly at Norman when we were there, only when she was reminding him about 'the mix-up in aisle 12' – a business matter. And when she brought the tea-tray, she touched his arm as she put it down on the desk, and he patted her hand in return! Both of these could be seen as intimate acts. And that says nothing about the smug expression on her face as she left the office! 'Here I am – acting as a hostess for Norman!' And, he said 'dear' to her once – it all adds up if you are in the know."

Replied Alex, "If you say so, that is enough for me, my darling. So, does this little liaison have anything to do with the main event? Maybe we should set it aside and try and find more about the background to the attempted sabotage. What about your observations at the pub yesterday? I am very intrigued by the three men you caught surreptitiously studying a piece of paper, could we investigate that further, perhaps? And maybe Will Brooks has spent enough time in the cells by now to soften him up a bit. Did Stephen say when he is due to come up before him today?" "No, but if we were to call at the court on the way home, there is probably a running-list of cases we could see. Shall we try?"

They parked just down the street from the courthouse and went into the building. Melpomene approached an attendant and asked him if there was a schedule for the court that she could see. "Well, yes, Miss – there it is over there on the notice-board, but Major Buckmaster has called a lunch adjournment now, and the court won't be in session again until about 1 o'clock."

"Where does the Major take lunch on these occasions, we would like to speak to him if we may?" asked Melpomene. "Why, just round the corner in the Lilac Tea-Rooms," said the man, "but he has his clerk with him, so he may not want to be disturbed."

"We can but try!" was her reply. They went over to the noticeboard and saw that there were six or seven entries ticked off, and then a line drawn across. Alex read them out, "Two shopliftings, one offensive behaviour, taking away a bicycle without the owner's consent, two more shopliftings and a drunk in charge of a horse and dray. Our bird comes on straight after the lunch adjournment: 'Being found on private premises in the company of others, with the intent to commit a felony.' My word!"

In the Lilac Tea-Rooms, an establishment which came up to its name in every respect, they saw Stephen Buckmaster enjoying what looked like fish and chips, in earnest conversation with a young man with a wispy moustache and thick glasses.

Melpomene approached his table and said, "If you are busy, Stephen, please tell us so, otherwise we would like a word or two." "Why hello Melpomene and Alex, may I introduce my clerk, Mr Simmonds? – Mr and Mrs Crabbe. Actually, we had finished our business, now, so please join me, by all means. Thank you, Simmonds, I'll see you back in court."

A waitress came and hovered with her pad, and Stephen said, "I can recommend the sole and chips, but if you want something lighter, the salads here are excellent." They both agreed to the sole.

After they had sampled the fish, which was indeed very good, Melpomene broached the business of their visit. "Well Stephen, we think we know why Will Brooks and his cohorts were at the mill – they were engaged in sabotaging the looms. Fortunately your interruption meant that they only had time to get at one of them."

"Thank you for that, Melpomene, I was wondering myself, but that sounds very likely indeed, which means they were put up to it by someone. I will try and extract some information from him this afternoon, but when criminals work in collaboration, it is often very hard to get them to talk, since they are more afraid of retribution from their associates than they are of our comparatively mild judicial sanctions. We shall see!"

Chapter 8

Melpomene and Alex found a seat at the back of the court, well before one o'clock. On the hour, the clerk announced, "All rise, Major Stephen Buckmaster, presiding Magistrate." Stephen took his seat and then nodded to Simmonds, who said in a clear voice, "Call William Henry Brooks." Will Brooks was led up stairs into the dock and the proceedings began with the clerk establishing that the accused was who he was meant to be.

Stephen rapped his gavel and started to address the accused, but before he had said much more than his name, a man in barrister's dress, with a wig, stood up in the front row of seats and said, "If it please the court, I am Stanley Jerrold, KC, representing the accused Brooks, and I request that this case be immediately referred to the County Court."

"On what grounds, Mr Jerrold?" enquired Stephen, to which the reply was, "My client needs time to assemble his case, and I have information that others have an interest and also need time to prepare."

"This seems extraordinary – you have not yet heard any details of the charge to be laid. Is your instructing solicitor present in this court, Mr Jerrold? If so, I will see him and yourself in my chambers – immediately, if you please!" and he turned and swept out through his door while the clerk was still saying, "All rise!"

Simmonds, too, disappeared through the magistrate's door, and emerged less than five minutes later to announce that the court was closed for the day, and that everyone should go home. Brooks was led down the stairs again.

Melpomene turned to Alex, saying quietly, "Did you recognize the instructing solicitor? I could swear he was one of the three men that I saw in the pub yesterday, with the mysterious paper! I think he was the one called Vince. We can ask Stephen about him later, I hope! But I suppose he will go straight home this evening, and we can hardly disturb him there, can we? We may as well go back to the hotel, now, I suppose."

They got back into the Alvis, Melpomene insisting that it was her turn to drive, and started to make their way back to the main highway. But then Alex pointed out a couple of young girls waiting at a bus-stop, carrying shopping-baskets. "Isn't that Phoebe Buckmaster?" he said, so Melpomene pulled up just past the stop. She called out, "Do you want a lift, Phoebe?" and the two girls eagerly came up, Phoebe saying, "Oh, yes please, we think we just missed the bus – have you got room for both of us, this is my friend Janice – Mr and Mrs Crabbe, Janice!"

Alex got out and went round to open up the dicky-seat, saying, "It's not very big, but will certainly be enough for two slim creatures, if they hold their shopping on their laps! Where are you heading? Do you want us to take you home?"

"Oh, yes please! Janice is staying with us until the end of the holidays – we both go to the same school. If you take the next left turn, I will guide you."

"Hold on to your hats!" said Melpomene, "Your school panamas will catch the wind once we get going!"

"Yes, we only wear them because Mummy insists – she says we need to protect our complexions!"

They were soon driving in through the gates of a substantial house in an affluent district of Woodhampton, and they were followed up to the front door by a smart green saloon, out of which stepped Stephen Buckmaster, saying, "Hello girls, and greetings, Mel and Alex! I hope my daughter didn't harass you into giving her and her friend a lift! Now you're here, you must come inside for a drink and a chat, if you have the time."

Once in the hallway, the two girls headed for the kitchens to deliver their groceries, and Stephen ushered Melpomene and Alex into a comfortable sitting room, with lush carpets and the sort of chesterfields often seen in a gentlemen's club. He sat them down and then pressed a bell-push. A smartly-dressed maid appeared and Stephen said, "Would you like some tea and cakes – I'm sure we have some nice ones, haven't we, Hetty?"

"Oh, yes, sir. And I think the young ladies will have brought some Kunzle cakes, too, if they could get them at Middleton's. China or Ceylon tea would it be? The mistress told me to say she would be joining you in a moment, as soon as she'd powdered her nose!"

"So, wasn't that a lot of fun in court today!" said Melpomene when the maid had gone, "What are we to make of it, Stephen? We have seen that instructing solicitor before, you know."

"Oh, have you? That is interesting – you must tell me all about it – to tell the truth it is most unusual for a small-time offender to be represented at all, so I have been wondering whether both he and the barrister had been engaged by an interested third party. But first I will let you in on what transpired with him and Jerrold in my chambers – there's nothing confidential about it, and you might be able to make use of the information in your enquiries."

Just then, Eugenie came in, closely followed by Hetty, who set the tray down on a small table, curtseyed and left the room.

Eugenie kissed Melpomene on both cheeks and shook Alex's hand, saying, "So it's beginning to look as though I was right to suspect sabotage, don't you think?"

"Yes, my love," said Stephen, "and when I tell you what that barrister had to say, you will be even more convinced. He had the effrontery to suggest that Brooks was being set up – by whom he did not say – and that he was being played as a pawn by powerful commercial interests. I could tell that this harangue bothered Vincent Greene, the solicitor, who would have liked to shut Jerrold up, I think. I've known other barristers in the past, particularly young ones, who had a tendency to go off half-cocked – some of them out of a sense of superiority over the humble solicitor."

"So what was all of this to do with having the case heard elsewhere?" asked Alex, "I can't see the reasoning here yet."

"Well, of course, he would not say so in as many words, but the implication was that everyone in Woodhampton – including me as a part of the local judiciary – would naturally have a stake in Gormsby's as an important employer and source of profit to the town, and would be inclined to take sides accordingly."

"But I can see a flaw in this reasoning," said Melpomene, "neither Brooks, nor indeed, Norman Felton, are locals, so why would they be thinking in that way? Perhaps Jerrold was not aware of this."

"Or perhaps there is more in it than meets the eye!" was Alex's final comment on this.

Chapter 9

"By the way, Stephen," asked Alex, "what is happening about the two lads that were found in Gormsby's with Brooks?"

"Well, as juveniles, they have been remanded in the custody of their parents until the next sitting of the Children's Court, in a week or so. I have the dubious honour of presiding over that court too, but as one of a panel of three – my companions being Miss Anabelle Higgins, the matron of the local cottage hospital, and, my dear Melpomene, your esteemed Aunt, Lady Isabel Musgrave! By the way, Melpomene, I have been wondering for a while why you do not use the appellation 'The Honourable' – you must be entitled to it, surely, since your Mama is a Lady, and your late father was Lord Musgrave?"

"You are quite right, Stephen, of course. Alex would be tickled to be openly married to an Hon, I'm sure – but he is too much of a gentleman ever to say so! I am holding that title in reserve, and I shall have no hesitation in bringing it out if it ever appears likely to give us an advantage in one of our cases. But, in these modern times, I feel that titles are merely relics of the middle ages, when the monarch would hand them out to whosoever had brought him lands, or profit, or won him a battle. I don't believe my own ancestors were knaves, of course, but there are skeletons in many a noble closet to this day!"

"What Mel doesn't know, perhaps – though maybe she does, at that" said Alex, "is that I frequently drop her title when I'm at my club, or talking to my legal colleagues. It is my view that anything is justifiable that will give us an edge in our legal or investigative pursuits! I myself have no hesitation in calling upon the good will of old boys of my school or of university acquaintances."

"Aha!" said Eugenie, "We have here a couple of dark horses – but only in the service of truth and justice, I'm sure! Any more of these delightful cakes, anyone?"

Melpomene took up her offer, saying "Ooh, I really like these marzipan ones – stop me someone or I shall not have room for dinner!" Alex chuckled fondly, "If you listened to Mel you would think she was in imminent danger of becoming rotund – actually she has the constitution of a pigmy shrew, which, I'm told, starves if it doesn't eat every two hours. But, of course, she is by no means shrewish in other respects."

"Just in time, Alex, just in time! Had you not added that last remark, you and the others would have found out that I can be just as waspish as the next person!"

The pair soon took their leave, and as they drove away, Alex at the wheel this time, Melpomene said, "Tell me what you think, Alex, about this idea. I would dearly like to talk some more to Miss Elsie Pickford, but it would be nice if a casual meeting could be contrived. Do you know when the shift finishes at Gormsby's?" Alex thought a bit, "Didn't Norman Felton say that they started at 8 am? That would mean that, assuming an eight-hour shift, they would knock off at 4, or 4.30 perhaps if they are given a lunch break. We could accidentally be driving past the gates then and see. But even so, we would need some reason to talk to Elsie, wouldn't we?"

"Mm, I get your point, Alex. Let me think! What time is it now – a quarter to 4 already if my watch is right? Why don't we drive to the mill, and I will dream up an excuse as we go."

As they drove past the gates, they could see the gatekeeper standing there, maybe getting ready to control the workers as they came out. "Pull up, Alex, and I'll have a word with him," said Melpomene, "he may recognize us from our earlier visit."

She got out and strolled over to the man, who straightened up and saluted as she arrived. "An ex-soldier, I would say," thought Melpomene, "maybe I can take advantage of this."

"Good afternoon, Sergeant is it?" He swelled a little, "Sarnt-major, actually, Ma'am, late of the Royal Gloucesters, at your service."

"All I wanted to know, Sergeant-Major, is when the troops knock off this afternoon."

"No problem, Ma'am, the girls come out on the stroke of 4, and the men at 4.30 pip emma – they has a longer shift, you see, being men."

Just then a hooter sounded in the mill, and the gatekeeper, looking at his watch, said, "Here they come now!"

Some were picking up their bicycles from the racks behind the gate-house, and riding off in ones and twos, while others streamed out to bus-stops, one each side of the road. The bus headed away from town arrived first, and a dozen or so girls boarded it before the clippie, standing on the back platform, rang the bell for it to depart. Melpomene had tried to keep a watch on them, but she couldn't be sure whether Elsie was in that group.

She wandered up to the queue that had formed at the other stop, where the girls were chattering and laughing together and looked along the line, but couldn't see Elsie there either, so returned to the Alvis, shaking her head at Alex. "No luck, eh?" he said as she got in. Then the townbound bus arrived and bore its load to Woodhampton.

Then Melpomene, looking back at the factory gates, said, "Hang on a moment, Alex, there's a couple more." Indeed there was, a man walking with the elusive Elsie, who was obviously displeased about something, and was almost shouting, "Now look what you've gone and made me do, Eric Watson, I've missed me bloody bus and I shall have to wait for the men's bus and put up with all sorts of cheek all the way into town!"

"There's no call for that sort of talk, Elsie," he said, "I never forced you to stay and talk to me! If I could double you up on me bike, I would, but I don't go your way, do I?"

Then Melpomene called out, "Elsie Pickford isn't it? Do you remember us from when you were having a quarrel about lost heddles this morning? We can give you a lift into town, if you don't mind squeezing into the dicky-seat."

Elsie looked hard at her, and then remembered and said, "Oh, thanks ever so much, you wouldn't believe what a trial it is for a girl to travel with a bunch of weavers!"

Melpomene opened the dicky-seat and helped her to climb in, saying "Better take off your hat and hold it, or it'll blow away for certain! You can tell us where you want to go as we drive – we're in no particular hurry this afternoon."

Before long the Alvis caught up and passed the bus, and Elsie made much of waving to her workmates as they sped by. "That'll give 'em plenty to talk about – I shall get no end of a ribbing at work tomorrow, but I don't care, it'll be worth it!" She laughed happily and nearly forgot her turn-off, but then pointed out her house in a long terrace of identical modest workers' houses.

Chapter 10

"Will you come in?" said Elsie, "Me mum would be proud to give toffs like you a cup of tea!"

Melpomene thanked her and then murmured quietly to Alex, "I shall have to write another methodological paper for a social anthropology journal, on the use of tea-drinking in research." "And yet another on the value of giving lifts to experimental subjects!" added Alex.

Inside the house, they were met in the hallway by Elsie's mum, who greeted them politely, while looking a little puzzled at Elsie's description of them as "A lady and gentleman what are doing some detecting at the mill." She took them into a room with unmatched easy chairs, a rather elderly-looking piano and a single occasional table. The room had the appearance – and slightly dusty smell – that betokened a rarely-used 'best' room.

Mum said, "Take a seat, please do, sir and madam, and we'll go and make a pot. I think we might have some nice biscuits, too!" She took Elsie's arm and bustled her away, presumably to ask her what this was all about!

In a few minutes they were back, Mum carrying a huge teapot dressed in a crocheted cosy, with a little pom-pom on top, and Elsie bearing a tray with cups and saucers, a milk jug, a sugar basin and a slop-basin, all the crockery in a matching design. Melpomene thought that they must indeed be honoured guests to be granted the use of the best china.

They were soon all nursing their teacups and nibbling biscuits. Alex opened the discussion, as he and Melpomene had decided.

"Miss Pickford," he said. "Oh, please call me Elsie!" said she. "So, Elsie, as you know, we came down to your aisle this morning because you and that weaver, Steve Briggs, were having a set-to about missing heddles. From what we saw and heard, Elsie, we can tell that none of it was your fault. We already know that Will Brooks was caught in the mill on Sunday, with a couple of kids, up to some sort of mischief, so the most probable explanation is that he was messing about with the looms, taking the heddles and spoiling the warp. Who knows how many set-ups they would have ruined between them if they hadn't been caught."

Melpomene took over, "You know that Will Brooks was up before the magistrate today about being caught in the mill – we were both in court, and can tell you that nothing was found out, because some interfering lawyers piped up before he could be questioned. So he has been put on ice until he can be tried again properly so that he can give his side of the story. Alex and I think that Will Brooks is being taken advantage of – maybe by some big company who want to ruin Gormsby's – and probably put all you workers out of a job, setters and weavers alike. We heard that you have sometimes been friendly with Will, so we wondered whether you had any ideas about what he has been up to, or who has been getting at him."

Elsie thought a moment and then said, "Well that's right, Will and I did walk out together a couple of times – nothing serious, just friendly-like – but he never said nothing about nobody asking him to do owt like that. I was as surprised as the others when we were told he was caught – Arthur Watson, the caretaker, has been going round telling everybody how he single-handedly caught this desperate gang – he doesn't say nothing about the police helping him out, o'course!"

"Thanks, Elsie, that's very interesting!" said Alex, "While we're here, perhaps you can put us straight about something else. Since Will was collared last week for having a bust-up in the street, people have been saying that he was just trying to take somebody's gun away in case anybody got hurt. Is that right, or is it just a made-up story?"

"No, it's true – some of 'em at the pub saw Paddy O'Brien take his gun out as everyone left the public at closing time. Jim Webster allus makes sure they all get out in good time – I think he was done for after-hours drinking a couple of times a few years back. Well, if you ask me, Paddy wasn't going to threaten nobody – he was a bit pissed – oh sorry, Miss, drunk I mean – but he's a quiet man who never gets excited much, after all he's a poacher, so he knows how to keep calm – it didn't mean nothing, he was just shifting it before he got on his bike, and anyway, he never carries it loaded. Maybe I'm wrong, but I think Will Brooks got the wrong idea in 'is 'ead about Paddy and me. But me and Paddy hadn't been up to anything – we just talked a bit a couple of times is all – can't a girl talk to nobody?"

"Thanks for that, Elsie!" said Alex, and Melpomene added, "And thanks for the tea and bickies, Mrs Pickford – sorry if

29

we've caused any upsets, but we're in a business that makes us inquisitive, so we're always asking people all sorts of questions! I'm sure it'll all get sorted out in time – and I don't believe your Elsie is involved in any way!"

Melpomene was driving this time, and on the way back to the hotel she said, "I'm dying for a proper cup of tea – the good Mrs Pickford's was stewed and strong enough to take the enamel off one's teeth! By the way, to you as a lawyer, how did Miss Pickford's evidence stand up?"

"Not badly, Mel, actually! She wasn't evasive, and I didn't spot any inconsistencies. I've seen much more muddled and shifty witnesses in court! So, what would your view be – what else do you look for in terms of social anthropology?"

"Well, my love, I was looking at the mother as much as at Elsie, and paying attention to any interactions between them, as well as to her words, of course. Mum showed nothing but pride in her clever daughter, for the most part. Loom setting is a skilled occupation and it not every young girl who would be able to do it. And Elsie never seemed to steal little looks at her mother, to check whether her story was going down well with her, as she might do if she were making it up as she went along. So, like you, Alex, I'm inclined to believe her!"

"So altogether," said Alex, "we're not much forrader, are we? We still don't know whether Brooks is being got at, or who might be getting at him."

"But at least," replied Melpomene, "we have nothing to the contrary, Alex. I'm inclined to proceed on the assumption that there is such a malign influence lurking somewhere about. I think we've extracted as much as we can from the mill workers and management for the moment, so why don't we turn our attention to your legal colleagues, Messrs Jerrold and Greene? My instinct is that these two are deeply involved in any plot that is going! But how are we going to approach them, we don't even know where their base is, unless Stephen was given any particulars. And, since I am a cunning, devious woman, I made a mental note of Stephen's home telephone number while we were in his house! I must write it down before I forget."

"Well, it's probably in the telephone directory, anyway, Mel!"
"No it isn't, I already looked! He probably wouldn't want crank calls to his home, in his position!"

Chapter 11

Back at the hotel, Alex was just about to try Stephen's home number when he had a better idea. "I should have the numbers of the Law Society and the Bar Council in my little book, Mel – I can just ring them and ask the respective registrars about Messrs Greene and Jerrold. Here I go, wish me luck!"

The hotel telephone was in a small room off the main lobby, with a chair that Melpomene swiftly appropriated, while Alex stood at the instrument, picked up and asked for the number he had written in his notebook. The operator said, "That is a London number, Sir, and there will be a toll charge – will you accept that?" Soon he was speaking to the Law Society registrar, identified himself as a solicitor – there was a pause, while apparently his bona fides were being checked – and was soon given the details of Vincent Greene.

He wrote them down in his book and then told Melpomene, "He is listed as having an office in Whitechapel – that alone tells us that he may not be particularly reputable, although one should not condemn a man for practicing in a low-rent district, I suppose!"

"Certainly not, Alex! Let us wait until we have dug into his murky activities before doing that! What about Jerrold?"

Alex went through a similar procedure and then informed Melpomene, "He shares chambers in Gray's Inn, but the Bar Council registrar said he could not divulge any more than that, but that I might make enquiries of the Inn clerks there. He gave me a telephone number, but I think we'd better do some more planning before we try it."

"Well done, Alex! That is a very good start. Are there any publications we could peruse to see what cases these two have been involved in?"

"For that, we would have to go through Law Reports – when a student, I can remember ploughing through heaps of such documents in the University College law library – and, of course, as an ex-student I could still do this!"

"So, my love," said Melpomene, "it looks as though we had better head back to London quite shortly! But not until after dinner, please! Why don't we go tomorrow morning?"

After another of the hotel's substantial breakfasts, Alex and Melpomene, wrapped once more in dustcoats, took the A-road towards London. There was a light drizzle, and Alex, who was driving, said, "I think we'd better try and avoid streets with trams, Mel, our dear Alvis doesn't get on well with wet tramlines, I think because the wheel track is close to the same width as them. But we can't really avoid going through Blackwall tunnel – it doesn't have trams, but the horse traffic tends to leave, shall we say, a treacherous surface sometimes!"

"I'm confident you will be able to manage, Alex. We are in no particular hurry – shall we go home first, or straight to the office?" "Office, I think, then we can make some more enquiries – I'd like to check with University College before we go to the library there. It could have different opening hours over the long vac."

Within a couple of hours, they were in Greenwich, driving along Tunnel Avenue and heading into Blackwall tunnel, where they spotted a couple of uniformed men with barrows, engaged in removing Alex's 'treacherous surface'. Leaving the tunnel, in twenty minutes or so they had passed through the dock areas and what Mel referred to as the 'notorious Whitechapel' and were in Finsbury Park, pulling up in a laneway between the shops on the ground floor of the building which housed their little office on the third floor.

They paused before their front door, admiring the gilt lettering 'Crabbe and Crabbe – Private Investigators', opened the door and went in, to be greeted by their slightly surprised receptionist/secretary, who jumped up and said, "Oh, Miss Melpomene and Mr Alex, I didn't know you were coming back so soon!"

"That's all right, Marjorie, come into the inner sanctum and we can all catch up with what we've been doing. Any chance of cups of tea?"

"Oh yes, and I've got some of your favourite jam tarts – Mrs Jenkins made a fresh batch this morning, and I bagged a dozen before she could sell them all!"

"You first, Marjorie!" said Alex when they were all sitting in the inner office with their teas and jam tarts, "Have any new clients approached us? And what happened with the Misses Atwell?"

"Nothing new, I'm afraid, but Agatha Atwell has finally admitted that she forged the codicil. Miss Emmeline will not press charges against her sister, and your cheque is in the mail, she says. I shall make sure it is deposited as soon as it arrives! Meanwhile, I have been trying to make sense of your files, Mr Alex, and I think I have worked out your system at last!"

"As a reward, Marjorie, you can call me Alex! Now I'll tell you a bit about our adventures in deepest Hampshire!"

He and Melpomene proceed to relate all that had happened with Gormsby's mill, and Marjorie took notes, saying, "We shall risk forgetting a lot of this if we don't record it, you know. Once the business has grown a bit, we shall need an orderly set of files, as I found out when I was working for old Mr Hamilton at Hamilton, Hamilton and Dykes. Do you want me to approach this Mr Greene, or his secretary if he has one? From what you have just said, he might recognize both of you straight away, and get suspicious."

"Good point, Marjorie!" said Melpomene, "Actually I was rather thinking that I could go to see him somewhat disguised, since he couldn't have got much more than brief glimpses of me at the pub or in court. I'll think about it some more – we really have to have a clear idea what we want to find out about him before we commit ourselves to action."

"What I was thinking," said Alex, "was that one of us might approach him with some sort of dodgy proposition and see how he reacts. Of course, if he doesn't take the bait, we would be no wiser. And Jerrold is another kettle of fish altogether – since a barrister doesn't deal directly with clients in the first instance, we might have to get to him through Greene."

"Don't forget we planned to see if we could find anything of interest in the Law Reports," Melpomene pointed out, "let's see what we can come up with at the University College library, first. If we find anything that smells, we can take things from there."

As they got up, Melpomene saying that they should do a bit of shopping before they went home, Marjorie said, "I don't know about you two – have you forgotten that we have been subscribing to the Fortnightly Law Digest for the past nine months? There might be something interesting in that, mightn't there? I'll go through it straight away, now I know a few names and facts – and I'll look out for any cases to do with factories."

Chapter 12

It was only a five-minute drive from the office to the Crabbe's house, in a quiet side street off Liverpool Street, not far from the main railway terminus, but they needed to do some shopping en route, because they had given the housekeeper, Mrs Mountain, and Caroline, the housemaid, a few days off while they were in Woodhampton, and they were not due back for two more days. They parked the car on the street and, carrying the shopping between them, went up the six front steps and unlocked the door. Stepping inside, they had to avoid a pile of mail that had been posted through the letter-slot.

"Phew!" said Melpomene, "Open some windows, please, Alex, the house gets stuffy when it's closed up in this warm weather. Let's be informal and eat in the kitchen, I don't feel like laying the dining table just for a scratch meal."

They carried the groceries into the kitchen and set them down. "I'll boil a kettle first," said Alex, "I imagine you are ready for another cup of tea!" Melpomene crossed to the dresser, where there was a large wireless set, she switched it on, and waited for it to warm up. "What time is it, Alex?" she said, "Five to six? There should be a BBC news broadcast at 6 o'clock."

Indeed, they soon heard the six pips heralding the news, and the announcer's voice. "This is London calling. It is six o'clock and here is the news. There has been a gruesome discovery this morning in the county prison in Andover, Hampshire. When the warder made his usual rounds, waking the prisoners up to mop out their cells and go for their breakfast, there was no answer from one of the cells occupied by a remand prisoner, William Henry Brooks, bachelor, aged 41, of Woodhampton, Hants. He was lying in his bed and was subsequently found to be dead. Investigations as to the cause of death are proceeding. And now to other news …"

Melpomene gave a little cry and clung to Alex' shoulder, "How can we find out more, Alex? Should we phone Stephen Buckmaster?"

"Let's try, Mel, but it's highly likely he will be busy on this case. Give me his number and I'll see whether I can get him."

Alex went into the hallway, picked up the telephone and asked for the number. After a few minutes he heard a young female voice, saying "Hello?" so he said, "Is that Phoebe? This is Alex Crabbe, is your father home?"

"Hello, Mr Crabbe, no he's not here, neither is Mummy, but I bet I know what you are phoning about, I can tell you what little I know, if you like – I was around when Daddy was talking to the superintendent and to Mr Felton about it. I don't think they'd mind if I passed it onto you."

"Yes, please go ahead, Phoebe, as long as it doesn't upset you."

"Not at all – after all, I never met Mr Brooks. Superintendent Wilkinson phoned Daddy, it must have been about 10 o'clock – he had just got the news from the prison. Since Daddy had been involved with the arrest, the Superintendent suggested he take him to the prison in his police car. He was picked up about twenty minutes later, and he was away for over three hours. When he came back, he said he couldn't stay long, as he was going to talk to Mr Felton at the mill, but he told us that a doctor had looked at Mr Brooks but said it needed a full post-mortem to establish the cause of death, as there was nothing apparent as far as he could see. This was Dr Hookham, I've actually met him once – he's the Police Surgeon, so I should think he knows about these things. And that's about all I can tell you, Mr Crabbe. Would you like me to ask Daddy to phone you when he gets back? Just tell me your telephone number and I'll write it down."

"Yes, thank you, Phoebe, you have been wonderful! Our number is Finsbury 1692. We shall be here all this evening."

He put down the phone and turned to talk to Melpomene, who was holding out a glass of whisky. "Oh, thanks, Mel, I could do with that – what a shock – are you alright, love?"

"Oh, yes, Alex, I'm not upset, but my head's whirling, thinking what we should do next. If Greene and Jerrold have heard about this – which is certain, since it was on the news – they will be extremely wary of anyone making any sort of enquiries, even if they are apparently nothing to do with the unfortunate Brooks. So, I think we are forced to confine our efforts to looking up the records. Is Marjorie on the telephone at home? If we can get her, let's tell her we'll go to the Law Library tomorrow morning and then compare notes with her back at the office in the afternoon, what do you say?"

"That sounds good, Mel, now let's have something to eat, I'm famished with all this excitement, and my jam tarts are long gone!"

They left the wireless playing quietly, in case there might be more interesting bulletins, and fried up a large pan of eggs, bacon, mushrooms and fried bread, accompanied by several more cups of tea.

"This is not a proper meal, but after all, these are emergency conditions!" said Melpomene.

At about 10 pm the phone rang. It was Stephen, of course, and he had much of interest to impart to them.

"No more medical reports on the victim, yet – we are not promised anything until tomorrow morning at least, since they are analysing stomach contents and so forth. But this has really put the wind up Norman Felton – he thinks that this whole affair is turning out to be much more serious than we all thought at first. So he has asked for special police protection for the mill, and also for him and his wife at home. And, though he is being rather secretive about it, I have come to the conclusion – shared by Wilkinson, by the way – that he has recruited some of his burliest weavers as a sort of mercenary force, armed with cudgels, who will patrol the mill, inside and out, all night. I only hope they don't get out of hand in their enthusiasm – weavers have the reputation of being very hard men!"

Melpomene had been listening on the French-style second earpiece, and this information prompted her to make a further suggestion. "If I were asked to predict the actions of a crooked lawyer working in cahoots with some sort of gang, I would say that the news about Brooks would cause them some sort of action or reaction – according to the theories of group behaviour they would seek to draw together with other members in response to the perceived threat, especially if they got wind of defensive precautions at the mill."

"So what are you proposing?" asked Alex, "Keeping watch at Greene's office, or what?"

"That's right!" said Melpomene, "I can't think they would meet at the Inns of Court – much too public – so Greene's office – or a pub – is the best guess we have available, wouldn't you say? Of course I shall have to play it all by ear."

"And you do have a good ear, my pet!" said Alex.

Chapter 13

Alex thanked Stephen, said he would keep in touch, and hung up the phone. He turned to Melpomene and said, "Let me get this straight – are you seriously proposing to find Greene's office, lurk outside until Jerrold arrives, or till Greene goes to a pub to meet him, and then eavesdrop on their conversation, using your lip-reading skills? You realise that an attractive young woman, hanging around in the street in Whitechapel, will probably be taken for a prostitute, don't you? How will you deal with prospective clients, or with officious policemen moving you on, or even running you in? This is madness, Melpomene!"

"Oh Alex, ye of little faith!" retorted Melpomene, "How about the following scenario – a dear little old grey-haired lady, obviously respectable but fallen on hard times, is selling pathetic little bunches of violets outside the entrance of some offices. She even goes into these offices to try there, but is rebuffed. Eventually she spots Greene and follows him to his rendezvous!"

"You are in the wrong profession, my darling – you should be writing stories for ladies' magazines, or the romance books that shop-girls read on the Underground! Nevertheless, I think you might have something there. If I could lurk nearby, keeping watch, I would feel easier about it, but I don't think you would agree to that, independent person that you are! At least take your police whistle with you – it's a pity you haven't got a little handbag pistol!"

Melpomene laughed fondly and replied, "So we will talk more about our respective plans in the morning. I'm going to have a cup of chocolate and go to bed! Will you join me?"

She slept well that night, but Alex awoke around 4 am, tossed and turned for a while, thinking wildly, but then gave up and went to have a bath. When he returned to the bedroom, Melpomene was sitting up. "I heard the geyser start up," she said, "so I knew where you were. Make me a cup of tea, love, and then I'll get up too."

Over breakfast of porridge and tinned fruit, they discussed the morning's activities. "I'll ring Marjorie at the office about 9," said Alex, "then I'll try the Law Library at University College to see whether I can go there this morning. Are you still determined to masquerade as a flower seller? How do you propose to get to Whitechapel, do you want me to drop you discreetly somewhere near? I was going to go to the library by tube, but if you want to go to your destination by car, I can take you. I don't think you should take the Alvis yourself, because first, I don't want to leave it parked in Whitechapel anyway, and second, the sight of an old dear getting out of a flashy red sports car might cause a few raised eyebrows!"

Melpomene chuckled at the thought, "Don't worry, Alex, I'll take the underground, too. Us old flower sellers have to make do with public transport, when we've got enough pennies for a ticket, that is! And I don't know how the buses run in these areas."

"I'm going to rummage through Caroline's clothes to put together a suitable outfit, along with some of my own. I think Mrs M's would fit me like a tent, and I don't think Caroline would mind, as it's in a good cause!"

So, all going to plan, at about 10, they waved goodbye outside the house and set off in opposite directions to their tube stations. As she went, Melpomene practiced walking like an elderly woman, thinking that there was nothing more likely to spoil her subterfuge than striding out in her normal athletic style. At the station she purchased her ticket from a window, not being sure how to use the new ticket machines, and took the opportunity to practice a wavery old voice on the ticket seller.

Arriving at what she had worked out as the closest station to Greene's office, she made her way to the address she had memorised, which turned out to be a similar situation to that of Crabbe and Crabbe, offices above a row of shops. She took a deep breath and mounted the steps between a tobacconist and a fruit shop. There on the second floor, she saw a door with a wooden sign, "Greene and Mitcham: Solicitors and Notaries."

She knocked timidly and pushed the door open. Inside was a counter, with a fierce-looking woman apparently sorting papers. "Buy me lovely vi'lets?" she said, in her old woman's voice. "Not today, dear!" said the woman, not unkindly, and as Melpomene turned to leave, a door opened at the back of the room, and there was Vincent Greene!

38

"What is it, Sybil?" he said. It was apparent that he was somewhat nervous. "Just an old flower seller!" said Sybil "I've seen nothing of your colleague yet!" "Well let me know as soon as he arrives, do you hear!" said Greene, as he went back into his office.

Melpomene left, with her heart racing! She started down the stairs, and then saw that there was a bench outside some offices on the first floor, some sort of theatrical agency she thought, with a scruffy sign saying, "Global Productions. Ezekiel Partridge, Prop."

She sat down as a young woman popped her head out the door, "Are you here for the chorus call? Ah, no, sorry dear, I can see you ain't." "I'm just restin' me old legs!" said Melpomene, "That's all right!" said the woman, "take your time, my dear."

Melpomene waited and waited, There was a fair amount of traffic up and down the stairs, including three waifs who sat next to her on the bench, after checking in with Ezekiel Partridge. They were taken one at a time – the first two came out very soon, one with tears in her eyes, the other muttering a string of imprecations, but there was no sign of the third.

Melpomene formed the conjecture that she had been taken on for the chorus, but before she re-emerged, up the stairs galloped Jerrold, KC. And then, just as Melpomene was worrying that they would do their nefarious business in the office, they came down again, and to her delight, she heard Greene saying, "No, Stan, I want to keep off the beer until we get this sorted out. Let's go to Tony's coffee-shop, we can talk privately there."

Melpomene followed then down the stairs and was just in time to see that they turned left at the street. Now she took off her shawl and old ladies' bonnet, but retained her glasses, thinking that they would provide disguise enough. She gave her bunches of violets to a delighted little girl and found Tony's café a few doors along. It was not particularly crowded at that time of day, so once inside she looked round, and saw the two lawyers settling down at a table at the back of the room.

She selected a table that gave a good view of the pair, and ordered coffee and cakes from the waitress. She still remembered how to lip-read, from her University days visiting the school for the deaf, so even with the buzz of conversation she found she could follow what they were saying quite well. Jerrold started by asking, "Could they tell what killed him?"

Chapter 14

Greene snapped, "How would I know, I'm a solicitor not a medico! I suppose they will examine his organs, and analyse for all sorts of poisons, but I reckon there will be enough of that stuff in his body already that they won't be able to tell. The problem is that they must know I was the only one who visited him in jail – unless any relatives went."

"Or women!" said Jerrold, "He had the reputation of being a bit of a rough-hewn ladies' man, according to our friends, but I don't know whether they let non-family members in to see remand prisoners."

Then Greene did something that Melpomene had been concerned about, he put his head close to Jerrold, and whispered behind his hand. Jerrold reacted, shaking his head, "But he made it very clear that we should make no attempt to contact him unless he said so specifically – I'm certainly not game to cross him right now – I don't relish being dumped into the Thames in a sack!"

This idea seemed to unsettle the conspirators; they called for their bill, drained their cups and headed for the door. Melpomene could see that they separated outside the café, waving goodbye. She thought, "That's it for now – but there was interesting stuff there, anyway." She looked at her watch and decided to go back to the Crabbe and Crabbe office, since Alex might have left the law library by the time she could get to University College.

At the office, Marjorie looked up as she went in, saying, "Yes, Madam, how can I help you?" but then recognized Melpomene as she burst out laughing.

"I'll tell you all about it later, but right now, could you get me Superintendent Wilkinson, at Woodhampton police station please, as soon as you can. Meanwhile I'll go into the cloakroom and wash my face!"

Marjorie soon called her, "The superintendent is away from the station now; do you want to talk to Inspector Wright, who seems to be his second in command?"

"Yes, thanks, Marjorie, I'll take it in the office."

The inspector understood who Melpomene was and asked in what way he could be of assistance, saying, "I assume this is about the Brooks murder?"

"Yes, it is Mr Wright – so they've decided it is murder already, have they? Is there any way I can reach the doctor who has been doing the autopsy?"

"Well, Mrs Crabbe, I believe Dr Hookham is on his way back here with Superintendent Wilkinson, having done some tests at the Andover Hospital pathology laboratories near the jail. I haven't been told any specific results yet – I'm afraid that I may have jumped to conclusions about it being murder, sorry. As soon as they get in, I will tell them you called, and they will probably get back to you."

"Thanks, Inspector, I'm at Finsbury 5822, and will be here for some time."

She turned to Marjorie, saying, "Marjorie, do we have any reference books here that might have anything about poisons?"

"Not specifically, Melpomene, but I do have a couple of rather sensational books about famous trials and murderers that I picked up at a second-hand bookshop near here soon after I took this job – thinking then that the firm would be dealing with murders all the time – of course I have been disappointed up to now!"

"Oh, good, can I have a look? I don't suppose I'll find anything, but it will keep me occupied until Alex gets here. Oh, that reminds me, did you find any references to Greene or Jerrold in the Fortnightly Law Digest?"

"Yes I did, one or two, but I don't know how much use they will be. Greene seems to deal mainly with petty thefts and so on, and the only mention of Jerrold was to do with a breach of contract up North. I've put bookmarks in the relevant pages."

"That sounds good, Marjorie, but I'll look at your crime books first. And, of course, I'll need a cup of tea – Tony's coffee is not the best I've ever tasted – any jam tarts left?"

While Melpomene was nibbling a tart and sipping her Lapsang Souchong, she picked up one of Marjorie's books, 'Notable Murderers of Victorian England' whose lurid cover depicted a hanging, and started to look through the list of contents. She was struck by the title of one chapter, 'Arsenic and other

41

favourite poisons', finding that it dealt mainly with famous historical cases where the murderer was brought to book by the exhumation of a long-dead victim. A note at the end of the chapter caught her eye: '*The heavy metals, such as arsenic, antimony, mercury and lead are all highly toxic and can be detected in a body long after death. In strong contrast to these are the complex alkaloids, such as belladonna, hyoscine and nicotine, all of which are effective in low dosages and break down rapidly in the body. See: The Case of Dr Crippen, page 63.*'

She pondered this for a few moments and then turned to the chapter about stabbings and axe murders, but soon lost interest. "Where has Alex got to?" she asked nobody in particular. Then the telephone rang. Marjorie answered it and told the caller, "Yes, Mrs Crabbe is here, Superintendent, I'll put her on."

Melpomene took the instrument eagerly, saying "Oh, thank you for ringing, Mr Wilkinson, I'd certainly like to talk to you about all this, but first, may I ask if Dr Hookham is with you? Oh good, perhaps I might speak with him?"

The police surgeon came on, and Melpomene said, "I realise that you probably want to get on with your work, but I wanted to ask you a couple of questions. First, did your autopsy come up with an answer yet?"

Hookham replied, "Well, I'm still seeking second opinions from some of my professional colleagues, but my immediate answer is 'No, not yet,' I'm afraid. What was the other thing you wanted to know, Mrs Crabbe?"

"Please call me Melpomene, since we are almost associates now. What I wondered was this, did you notice the dead man's fingers and thumbs? Were they stained at all?"

"Well, as a matter of fact, they were heavily stained from smoking. Oh … I think I see what you are getting at! No, Melpomene, I didn't immediately think the results of my test for nicotine poisoning were significant, but of course, he may have had elevated levels if he was a heavy smoker! I'll ring up Dr Mason at the hospital – he was helping me with the p.m. and ask him to check another sample. This could turn out to be very interesting – Brooks did have his face contorted in a rictus, which could be consistent with a painful death!"

"Thank you, Dr Hookham – maybe we're on to something here – I never thought the poor soul died of natural causes!"

Chapter 15

Melpomene sat twiddling her fingers some more, and was just about to have another jam tart when Alex arrived. He was slightly surprised when she rushed into his arms and kissed him warmly.

"Oh, Alex!" she cried, "I would have burst if you had been any longer! Did you have any success with your research?"

"Yes, I did!" replied Alex, "But perhaps you should tell me about your adventures first, I can see you're dying to do that!"

So, over more cups of tea, Melpomene described what she had found out at Tony's and related her telephone conversation with Dr Hookham.

"It looks as though we are indeed onto our villains," said Alex, "but I'm coming to realise that Messrs Greene and Jerrold are merely bit players in this drama, and we shouldn't be too anxious to see them picked up by the police prematurely. What we need to do next is to discover the principal characters – and I think that I have found out something that might lead us to them!"

"Well, tell me, you beast! I can see you want to keep me in suspense!"

"I went back five years with the court reports and started scanning through, looking for 'Greene' or 'Jerrold'. There is a bunch of different 'Greene's and 'Green's, but even when I found our bird, there was nothing very interesting – petty thefts or traffic offences, that sort of thing – he doesn't appear to do conveyancing or inheritance stuff, but they wouldn't have been reported anyway, unless there was a dispute. Why anybody would engage a solicitor for such trivia, I don't know – but, come to think of it, I was quite grateful myself for half-guinea jobs when I was starting out! The only Greene case I made a note of was the one when he was associated with his current colleague, Jerrold. I'll tell you about that when I get to it."

"So," said Melpomene, "no serious crime, like burglary, or fraud? I'm thinking of this mysterious figure who has our pair scared of finishing up in the Thames – so how would they have met up?"

43

"Patience, my dear, patience! I'll come to it in a moment, but I'm trying to be systematic. Jerrold showed up in the reports less often than Greene, but, of course, as a barrister, he was associated with more substantial matters than Greene. The first case I thought had any relevance for us was a breach of contract about three years ago. I noticed it particularly because it involved a wool merchant and – wait for it – a firm of weavers! In Huddersfield, not in the West Country, though. But that was not the time when he was instructed by Greene."

"When they first worked together was in February this year, at Gloucester Assizes, which is getting a little closer to Ormsby's, geographically, anyway. The case was one of embezzlement – an accountant for a smallish engineering company had put his hand in the till to the tune of £40,000 over a two-year period. Apparently the embezzler knew Greene – from school, would you believe – the prosecutor made much of this, trying to denigrate Greene, I suppose. Jerrold's defence was to claim that his client had been put up to it by a director of the firm as a tax evasion manoeuvre, and had undertaken to return it to him after an agreed time. Strangely, the judge did not believe this, and threatened to report Jerrold to the Bar Council. There was no record in what I read of whether or not this had actually taken place."

Melpomene said, "That sounds sufficiently meaty that it might have made it to the popular press. Let's see!" She opened the door to the outer office and called out. "Marjorie! Feel like getting out of the office for an hour? If so, you could go to the local library and look through the back numbers of, say, 'The Banner' and 'The Trumpet' for a case. The hearing was on, what date, Alex? The 12th of February this year, so you could look at issues round that time, all right? We'll mind the telephone while you're gone."

"The case is 'Moorlands Engineering v. Simon Albert Blanche', at the Gloucester Assizes." Alex added.

"Right you are!" said Marjorie, putting on her hat, " 'The Banana' and 'The Strumpet', and I might try a couple of other papers if I get the chance." She grabbed her bicycle from the cloakroom and carried it down the stairs as though it weighed nothing.

Alex filled the kettle and put it on the gas-ring for another pot.

"We should work out what we should do to try and track down this sinister employer of Jerrold and Greene," he said. That manager in the embezzlement case sounds like a fairly shady character, but I think we need to look for someone deeper in the underworld, if the threat to our little friends was serious and not just bluster. Throwing people in sacks into the Thames sounds more like American hoodlum's tactics than London thugs, but they may have got their ideas from the pictures!"

"Jerrold certainly looked shaken!" said Melpomene, "And they both left Tony's in a panic."

"Did Marjorie come up with anything in the Fortnightly Digest?" asked Alex. "Oh, yes, I meant to look! Good job she is out, or she might be offended that I left it so long. There are the issues she found stuff in, on her desk, she's put markers in for the relevant pages. Let's see:"

Melpomene leafed through the journal, "Nothing much – nothing much – nothing much. The one you've already mentioned, the breach of contract in Huddersfield, was earlier than the issues we have. Aha! Here is Moorlands Engineering, but it doesn't look as though there is any more detail than we have seen already. Perhaps there will be something interesting in the newspaper. But here is a new one: only three weeks ago – of course the Fortnightly is more up-to-date than the main Law Reports."

"Can I see, please, Mel? What do we have here. *'Wimbledon Magistrates' Court. Rex v Cowlishaw, Bernard. Charge: house-breaking. Accused found in premises with a quantity of silverware. Jerrold KC, defending, stated that Mr Cowlishaw had been invited to take dinner with Miss Weems, the tenant of the property, and that he had been taking away some cutlery to have it repaired, plated and polished for the lady. Miss Weems stated that she had never met the gentleman before, and was not in the habit of inviting strangers to dinner. When the magistrate, Mr Desborough, asked Jerrold KC to comment on this, the barrister said, 'She's only a foolish old lady – she is probably confused.' Mr Desborough was not satisfied with this defence and sentenced Cowlishaw to a year's gaol with hard labour. He also berated Mr Jerrold and said his behaviour was not satisfactory for an officer of the court.'* My word, Mel, this man is certainly stretching things – the truth included, by the looks!"

The door opened and Marjorie wheeled her bicycle in. "I've got some good stuff!" she said, "I've written full shorthand notes!"

45

Chapter 16

Marjorie made herself a cup of tea and settled Melpomene and Alex down on the comfortable visitors' chairs in the office, then took out her notebook and began to read.

"Milk, bread, carrots ... whoops, wrong page! Here we are: 'Sensational Revelations in Embezzlement Trial! Peter Hamilton reporting. Before Mr Justice Wainwright, at Gloucester Assizes last Tuesday, Simon Blanche, 58, Accountant, of Wilmingham St., Cirencester, was accused of stealing as a servant the sum of £41,525, from his employers, Moorlands Engineering Ltd., of Hamley Road Gloucester, over a period of two years, starting in March, 1923. Adrian Bletchley, KC, for the plaintiff, said that Blanche had been placed in a position of trust by his employers, and given discretion over arranging invoices to large corporate customers of the firm, smaller amounts being dealt with routinely by other departments. It was one of these major customers, Arledge and Montgomery, a manufacturer of equipment for the textile industry, who first questioned one of these invoices, and upon a check by an independent auditor, Simpson and Associates, it was found that amounts had been falsified for a number of items billed. These adjustments could only have been made by Blanche, or with his knowledge. Subsequently a detailed audit was undertaken, which revealed the extent of Blanche's dishonest manipulations.'"

"Wow!" said Melpomene, "I wonder whether the firm also had dealings with firms like Gormsby's?"

"Hang on!" said Marjorie, "We haven't come to the meaty parts yet! I'll read on.

'The defence counsel, Jerrold KC, then rose and stated that the manipulations of the invoices had not been done for Mr Blanche's personal gain, but were at the behest of Sidney Poole, a director of Moorlands, in order to minimise taxes on the transactions, which were subject to profits tax – my lord, I can quote the relevant sections should you wish it – no, no Mr Jerrold, please continue –. My client took the instructions of his superior, Mr Poole, as direct orders, and merely obeyed them dutifully. The amounts were placed in a separate bank account under Mr Blanche's control for security reasons, and were to be returned to the firm at a later date, to be determined by Mr Poole.'

"There's more!"said Marjorie, gleefully, "Now we come to the nub of it!"

'Bletchley, KC, in reply, stated that the argument just advanced by the defence was nothing but a tissue of falsehoods. Bank records obtained by the Auditors, Simpson and Associates, reveal that the payments to Mr Blanche's secret account – by the way, my lord, the account was registered under a pseudonym, namely, S. White – my lord will readily realise that White is an English equivalent of the French Blanche or Blanc – yes, yes, Mr Bletchley, pray continue – that the payments to this account commenced on 14 March 1923, at a date when Mr Poole had not yet joined Moorlands, but was, in fact, working and resident in Zurich, Switzerland. He was invited onto the board of Moorlands only three months after that date. This, I submit, my lord, entirely destroys the defence case.'

'In rebuttal, Jerrold KC, stated that either Mr Bletchley had been duped or was lying through his teeth, that the auditors were obviously in cahoots with the management of Moorlands, and that his client, Mr Blanche was as honest as the day is long, unlike Mr Bletchley. At this point the judge ordered Mr Jerrold to be silent and sit down, which he did, muttering inaudibly the while.

'There was sensation in the body of the court while Mr Justice Wainwright retired to consider these submissions. When he returned, he struck his gavel and announced that Mr Blanche would be sentenced to a term of no less than five years, subject to appeal. Mr Jerrold begged leave to make a further statement, which the judge denied, saying that he had been gravely disappointed in the defence testimony and that he was strongly tempted to make a complaint to the Bar Council on the grounds of Mr Jerrold's unprofessional conduct. The case was adjourned as complete.'

Marjorie closed her shorthand notebook with a triumphant snap, and beamed at her audience, who clapped (Alex) and gave her a hug (Melpomene).

There followed intense discussion in the back office of Crabbe and Crabbe, Melpomene saying, "This Jerrold is obviously a thoroughly bad egg – but knowing this, what can we do with the information? What we have to do, first in importance, is to make sure that Jerrold and Greene are arrested for the murder of Brooks, and then to discover those behind the plot to ruin Gormsby's. The trouble is that the second would best be achieved while our two villains are still at large – once they are in custody it will be much more difficult to track down the master plotter."

"That means," said Alex, "that we should find out what has been happening with determining the cause of death, and what progress the police are making in identifying the killer or killers – if it does eventually turn out to be a murder. I myself have no doubt on that score."

"I think," said Melpomene, "that we should go back down to Woodhampton. Stephen Buckmaster, Superintendent Wilkinson and Dr Hookham are all there, and I think we should be talking to them without any further delay. They will be interested in what we have just found out, too. Marjorie, how long would it take you to type up your shorthand notes, and tidy up what Alex extracted from the records? Let's see, it's nearly four now, could you do it by five o'clock? Then we can set off for Hampshire first thing tomorrow."

"I can do that!" said Marjorie, "I was the fastest typist in my class at Pitman's College!"

"While you're doing that, I'll make some telephone calls," said Alex, "I'd like to find whether Dr Hookham has had the final results of his tests yet. I'll ring up Wilkinson at the station and see whether he knows, first."

Superintendent Wilkinson was called to the phone at the station, but he said that Dr Hookham had gone back to the hospital pathology lab. He gave Alex the number of the direct line, saying, "If you go through the hospital switch board they will want to know who you are, what is your business, etc, etc. I know from experience that this can take ages – but they're getting to know me now! Last I heard, Hookham was still waiting for the nicotine test to complete. I tell you what, all this has put me off smoking!"

Alex made his call, had a brief conversation, thanked the doctor and turned back to the others. "He can definitely confirm that the cause of death was nicotine poisoning! He reckons that a visitor gave Brooks a cigarette that had been doped with it – as soon as he started sucking on it, he would have ingested a fatal dose. Hookham said he would have suffered worse than from strychnine, and that is intensely painful! He recommends laudanum if you want to do yourself in!"

"Not at the moment, thanks!" said Melpomene with a shudder!

Chapter 17

Mrs Mountain not having returned, and Melpomene having exhausted all her cooking talents, they decided to go to a restaurant for a meal. Marjorie had finished her transcript, so Alex thanked her and stowed it in an inside pocket.

"Lord knows how long we'll be away this time, Marjorie. If there are any developments we shall be at the Castle Hotel after about mid-morning, so you can reach us there. Good night, and thank you for all this extra stuff today! Do you want to join us for dinner this evening, it'll only be at a modest place?"

"No, thanks very much, Alex, I'd better get home to my Mum! I'll see you when you get back to the teeming metropolis!"

Over dinner at a familiar little Italian place near their home, Melpomene and Alex discussed their next moves.

"Amongst everything else, Alex, I'd like to find out what is happening with the two kids that were caught with Brooks. I don't know whether they are still going to be charged at the Children's Court, but if they are, I might go to the hearing whenever it is, keeping a low profile, but with my ears open for anything useful they may be able to say. It will also be a nice chance to see my Aunt Isabel in action on the bench – I've never thought of her as an arm of the law!"

"But, more importantly, I am rather worried that whoever ordered Brooks to be murdered might think that these boys are a threat and have them disposed of too! I believe they are on remand at home in the custody of their parents."

"You know that Children's Court proceedings are normally not open to the general public?" said Alex, "You might have to do a bit of scheming to get in, even if your Auntie is on the bench! We could ask Stephen whether it is feasible. As for me, I would like to spend some more time talking with Norman Felton. I'm not trying to imply that he has been involved in any plotting, but he may know something that could help us to pursue some useful trails – after all, he must have many contacts in the textile industry."

"But before getting round to all that, I want to ask Superintendent Wilkinson whether there has been any success in determining who might have given Brooks the fatal dose. I suppose the prison authorities would have a comprehensive record of his visitors. My money, of course, is on Vincent Greene – especially since you actually heard him say at Tony's that he had visited Brooks in prison and was worried he would be suspected."

Melpomene nodded, but added, "I think you're right about Greene, but I must say I have taken a distinct dislike to friend Jerrold – he comes over, even in dry court reports, as a particularly nasty, vindictive, arrogant, dishonest bully! So it would give me great satisfaction to see him get his just deserts!"

"Now, now, Mel! You mustn't let your personal feelings get in the way of your professional approach!"

"I know, Alex, but it's therapeutic to have a bit of a rant now and then – and in general I know I can behave in the cool dispassionate way that I should!"

At about 9.30 the next morning, the Alvis drew up at the porte-cochère of the Woodhampton Castle Hotel, to be greeted once again by Mr Grimshaw and a staff member who unloaded their baggage.

"We didn't know you were coming, Miss Melpomene," said Grimshaw, "but be assured we will always be able to accommodate you and Mr Alex at whatever notice, or none!"

"My apologies for that!" said Melpomene, "We made the decision rather late this time. Where will you put us?"

"There's a nice suite on the first floor, Miss Melpomene, it was being occupied by Mr and Mrs Felton until yesterday, but they were called away on business suddenly, I believe. The concierge may have more information – I remember you had some dealings with them last time you were here."

Alex said, "I need to make some telephone calls – there is an instrument in our suite, I suppose?" "Oh yes, you will be connected directly to the local exchange, we don't have our own switchboard."

As soon as they had settled in their suite, Melpomene rang for tea and biscuits and Alex settled himself by the telephone, calling Stephen Buckmaster first. A woman answered, saying that he was in court already, as they had a full bill of cases for the day, but that she would ask him to return Alex' call when he had a half-hour adjournment for morning tea, at around eleven.

Alex next tried Superintendent Wilkinson, who answered straight away. After some chit-chat, Alex asked, "Have there been any further developments with the Brooks business – have they charged anyone yet?"

"Yes and no!" said Wilkinson, "It is now fairly clear that Brooks did die of nicotine poisoning – there were even blisters on his lips, which were missed on the first examination, Dr Hookham was a bit apologetic at overlooking that! Brooks had apparently been bundled into bed and covered up by the assailant – he still had one of his shoes on. But the police prosecutor, Inspector Bailey, of Hampshire County headquarters, is not prepared to make an arrest until more evidence becomes available, even though Vincent Greene is the only real possibility. Now, let me read you the notes that have been made so far in the prison daybook – they kindly sent me a copy of the relevant page – I won't bother with the times of the entries or the initials for the moment. Here we are."

'Visit by a Mrs Brooks, claiming to be spouse. Turned away as we knew Brooks to be a bachelor. Went away swearing, saying what about me money, then? Prison officer Jensen thinks she is a prostitute, known in the town.'

'Visit by Mr Vincent Greene, solicitor, claiming to represent Brooks. As interview room already occupied by Senior Prison Officer Phillips, PO Jensen and an alleged house-breaker, Greene allowed to interview Brooks in his cell. No officer available to stand in. Greene leaves after about twenty minutes, telling the officer who let him out that the prisoner had gone to sleep.'

'Prisoners called for cell cleaning and breakfast parade. Brooks failed to respond and was found apparently asleep. Senior officers alerted.'

Those are the only daybook entries that are relevant, Alex. But it does look as though progress is being made."

"Yes, this all very good, Superintendent. Do you know whether there have been any efforts made to interview Greene?"

"Yes Alex – please call me David – I telephoned the CID at the station nearest to Greene's office address, and asked them to find him and possibly interview him, and that I would send all the documentation we had so far. The officer I spoke with, Detective-Sergeant Manley, seemed to be a bright young man."

Chapter 18

Superintendent Wilkinson continued, "I said that if he located Greene, he should use his best judgment on whether to bring him in for questioning or just have him watched – I felt that if we kept an eye on him surreptitiously, we might stand a chance of getting a look at his underworld contacts. If and when DS Manley phones anything through, I will certainly let you know. Will you be at the hotel all day?"

"Not sure yet, David, I have some more calls to make, and I might decide to go and see Felton at Gormsby's. There are other possibilities too; Melpomene has plans of her own, I think. The hotel will take messages for us, of course. We're expecting Stephen Buckmaster to call during his court's adjournment for morning tea to give us his ideas. By the way, have there been any more developments with the two boys who were caught with Brooks? I understood they were placed in the charge of their parents."

"That's right, Alex, you know they're brothers, don't you? They are nephews of Brooks – his sister's kids, Tony and Sid Hoskins. Stephen had enquiries made around the neighbourhood before remanding them. It appears that they come from a decent family, but boys will be boys, and they have had several little run-ins with the police, scrumping apples and such – nothing leading to charges up to this time."

Alex thanked him and rang off. Turning to Melpomene, he said, "Enough of phoning – my ear is getting numb! Another cup of tea, and then if we haven't heard from Stephen, I vote for another visit to Gormsby's, unannounced this time. I don't really think we'll catch Norman at anything untoward, but the element of surprise can sometimes be worthwhile."

Stephen did ring at about 11 o'clock but said he couldn't add to what Wilkinson had already told them. They piled into the Alvis, putting the hood up because it looked like rain, and headed for the mill. The sergeant-major waved them through the gate, and they drove to where they had parked before. Next to Norman's Daimler there were two other cars, both large saloons, and there were two men, obviously chauffeurs, sitting on the running board of one of them, smoking and chatting.

Melpomene and Alex just nodded to them as they went up the iron stairs. In the main office, they were approached by a male clerk, who asked if he could help. When they said they were there to see Mr Felton, he apologized, "Mr Felton is talking with some businessmen in the conference room, but I believe that they are due to finish soon. Would you mind waiting? There are comfortable chairs in Mr Felton's office, we often put guests in there, and someone will make you coffee, if you like. Please come this way."

In the office, while sipping their coffee and munching on custard cream biscuits, Melpomene and Alex looked idly at the shelves of box files along one wall. They all had neatly-typed labels on their spines, and Melpomene drew Alex' attention to one she spotted, labelled 'Melinda Cartwright – Personal'. Next to it was another, 'Melinda Cartwright – Correspondence: Moorlands'. She asked Alex, "Wasn't that the name of the firm in the embezzlement case you turned up in the records, Alex?"

"I think so, Mel, it was 'Moorlands Engineering'. And I'm wondering if Melinda Cartwright is the same person as the current Melinda Felton – it's not a very common name, is it? Let's see if there are any other interesting-looking files."

They both scanned the shelves, and found one more that seemed to be related, labelled 'Moorlands: Disputed Contract'.

"My fingers are itching, Alex!" said Melpomene, "But even I wouldn't descend to reading files in someone's private office!"

Just then, the door opened, and Maureen appeared, exclaiming, "Oh hello, Mr and Mrs Crabbe, are they looking after you? I don't think Nor ... Mr Felton will be much longer. Excuse me, please." She went over to the shelves and took out a couple of box files, including, interestingly, 'Moorlands: Disputed Contract' and as she pulled it out she dislodged, but did not take, 'Melinda Cartwright – Correspondence: Moorlands'', which was shelved directly below. She hurried out again, not noticing the fallen file, which had come open and disgorged several documents.

"I shall tidy that up, Alex," said Melpomene, "but I shall scrupulously avert my eyes, lest I see anything confidential!"

"I applaud your ethical attitude, my dear, but I'm afraid my own ethics are overcome by my desire for information – maybe I shall just look at the front sheet of each of these documents, and if anything strikes my eye, well then that will not be my fault, will it?"

So, as Melpomene picked up each of them, she passed them before Alex' eyes until he nodded. He had taken out his notebook, and he made a few notes on each. As Mel was replacing the file on its shelf and they were settling themselves back in their seats, he passed her the book to have a look at.

"My my, Alex! I have known you so long and I didn't know you could write in shorthand! But it is not Pitman's is it – it looks nothing like Marjorie's – so what is it?"

"It is Gregg, Mel, we were actually taught it as part of the law course at UC – but I haven't used it much since – I rather surprised myself just now that I could still do it! We shall see later whether or not I can transcribe it!"

As he replaced it in his inside pocket, they could hear loud talking in the corridor outside. They could recognize Norman's voice, and there were two others, one a high, yapping, well-educated voice, while the other sounded rather lower class, with touches of cockney. As the latter left, he said, angrily, "When I tell the boss, he's gonna be upset, I reckon, so don't be surprised if he comes visitin' very soon!"

Then Norman came into the office, accompanied by Maureen, who was looking quite white. "Good afternoon, Mel and Alex!" he said, but it was apparent that he was having to work hard at controlling his tone, "To what do I owe the pleasure of this visit? That's all, Maureen, we'll talk about it later. Can I offer you any refreshments?"

"No, thank you," said Melpomene, "we have already had some coffee and biscuits and anyway it looks as though we picked an awkward time to call – we can come back later if you like."

Norman gave a big sigh, sat down at his desk and said, "I would get a big weight off my chest if I told you a few things right now – in complete confidence, of course. I have several times recently been at the point of unburdening myself, but I now feel I can be open with you – you seem to be trustworthy people!"

Melpomene shot a discreet grimace at Alex at that, but said, "Please go ahead, Norman, we're listening! Is it to do with the attempted sabotage at the mill?"

Chapter 19

Norman Felton now seemed close to tears, "Yes it certainly is about that!" he said, "But you must understand that I have been trying to stop them since the beginning! Let me start by explaining who my two visitors were just now, and I can gradually put the picture together for you. The first is Sir Ansett Browne, who is the chairman of the board of Winstanley Holdings, the owners of Gormsby's and two other mills in Huddersfield, woollen mills both of them. He seems implacably opposed to any actions that would affect the output and profitability of any of the mills, particularly this one. The other man, whose name I don't really know, is simply addressed as 'Osgood' by Sir Ansett – but he doesn't always respond immediately when addressed by that name, so I suspect it is an alias."

"He sounded very unpleasant to me!" said Melpomene, "I wouldn't be surprised to hear that he is some sort of crook!"

"My idea, too!" said Norman, "But I have the feeling that he is just a thug, whose job is to intimidate me and Sir Ansett. He doesn't seem to know much about the weaving trade – for instance, he keeps referring to 'spinning machines' when he means 'looms'. There must be bigger criminals behind him; he is just someone who carries out their orders. Who he works for, I have really no idea – I have to admit he worries me sick – he looks as though he could beat someone up and enjoy it."

"While I still have some information in my head, might I ring up Superintendent Wilkinson?" asked Melpomene. Norman simply nodded, and she picked up the phone on his desk and asked the operator for an outside line. She got through straight away, and said, "Melpomene here, David – I wonder if you could look up a couple of car numbers for me? TK 1126, and HF 1056 – I'll hang on if it's not going to take long." She turned to the others, saying, "I didn't know whether those two cars parked outside were important, so I memorised the numbers just in case!" And into the telephone, "Oh that was quick, David, let me write that down, 'Winstanley Holdings, Huddersfield' – that makes sense, I can look up the address if we need it – and the other, David? 'Feather, J.E., 27 Fillmore Gardens, Greenwich, SE 10' – that doesn't mean anything to me, I'm afraid. Can I try our acquaintance a little more and ask you to find out if there is anything in police records about anybody at that address, or about anyone called 'Osgood'? Oh, you're a treasure, David! I'll remember you in my will!"

She hung up and said, "Superintendent Wilkinson says he will give us anything he finds tomorrow! Please carry on with your account, Norman, I'm sure Alex is as agog as I am!"

Maureen, who had come back to the office a little earlier, and had been sitting with eyes like saucers up to that point, said, "Strange to say, I have seen this Osgood before!"

"Where was that?" asked Norman, "Here at the mill? And when?"

"No, not at the mill, in Woodhampton, a week or so ago. I'm pretty sure it was the same man – he was with another rough-looking type and they were walking along Market Street. I noticed them specially because they were just barging through the other pedestrians – one little boy was knocked over and grazed his knee, but they just ploughed on. A woman shouted after them, but they laughed and Osgood made a rude gesture – not a nice man at all!"

"So what did you think when he turned up today?" asked Alex.

"I didn't pay much attention to him at first – Sir Ansett always greets me affably, so I was responding to his polite little social enquiries. It wasn't until he started making threats that I had a good look and recognized him."

Melpomene spoke up, "Perhaps you could tell us more about this, Norman. Were these threats of physical violence or what?"

"No, much more like hints. It was very strange, really – Sir Ansett was making fairly indirect, even cryptic remarks, along the lines of 'You know, Norman, the textile industry is being affected by reduced demand. Some experts are even predicting that it will not be long before there is a widespread depression. We at Winstanley have been concerned for some time that our mills are not all performing at an ideal level.' ... and so on and so on. I formed the distinct impression that he was saying that if we at Gormsby's did not pull our socks up, so to speak, we might be shut down, as the group could only sustain two mills at the most. While he was going on like this, Osgood was working himself up to speak, and, just before they rose to leave, he said, 'So, Mr Felton, or whatever your name is, you'd better decide who is going down and who is going to fight. You've

56

already seen how it could be done! Only don't let your blokes get caught, or the same thing will happen what happened to Brooks! Are you going to play along or not?' That was when I protested that I would not do anything underhand and he stormed out!"

Melpomene went on, "I'm interested in whether you thought that Sir Ansett was really speaking on behalf of the Winstanley board, or whether there was some sort of hidden agenda, and that he was really the mouthpiece for some person or body lurking in the shadows."

"Well, I couldn't say for sure, but I did think a couple of times that he sounded as though he was reciting from a script. On other occasions he has been very voluble and long-winded, as though he was addressing a meeting, not just me. Perhaps today Osgood was there as a minder and prompter, so to speak!"

Alex said, "This is getting more and more interesting! Tell me, Norman or Maureen, why did they want the files that were fetched from this office?" "Oh, that was just my idea – I had thought I might point out some reasons for our output dipping in the past, but it turned out that they were not at all interested – I realised why as we went on, of course."

Melpomene and Alex looked at one another, and Melpomene said, "Thanks to Norman and Maureen, we have substantially increased the number of leads we need to follow up, now. So we had better go and leap into action. First stop, Woodhampton Police Station, I think – I for one have had enough telephoning to last me quite a while!"

"I beg to disagree, Mel!" said Alex, "In my opinion, the first order of business is luncheon! Where shall we go this time – not the Lilac Tea-Rooms, please!"

Norman had a suggestion, "Near the Market Square there is a nice little restaurant called Tessie's. It doesn't look much from the outside, but the lunches are excellent. Mention my name, I go there often!"

There was a small good-natured tussle over who should drive the Alvis and Melpomene won on this occasion. "Put the hood down, please, Alex, it looks as though it is fining up nicely!"

It took only a few minutes before they parked near Tessie's and pushed open the door, to be met with a delicious aroma.

Chapter 20

The restaurant lived up to Norman Felton's recommendation, offering a varied menu. Melpomene chose a Caesar salad, while Alex tucked into a mixed grill. "Please forgive me if I look away while you are eating the brains," said Melpomene, "I draw the line at lunching on what some creature has been thinking with!"

"Apropos of that", said Alex, "I was doing some thinking myself as we were driving here – when I wasn't praying, that is. It seems to me that we have been mostly concentrating on Brooks' murder and the possible motives for it – I have no real doubt as to the actual killer – and finding out who put Greene and Jerrold up to it, as well as whoever originally recruited the unfortunate Brooks – I think his nephews were probably his own idea. These are all important, but what we should really be doing is identifying the person ultimately responsible for employing these agents, as well as thugs like Osgood. With any luck, the leads we have picked up already might be useful, but I believe we need to broaden our approach. I would not be at all surprised were we to find the master-mind to be an eminent pillar of society."

Melpomene pondered this for a while, sipping her chilled white wine, and then said, "I'm with you on most of that, Alex – I don't know so much about the 'pillar of society' bit, although I wouldn't rule it out. What my training and experience incline me to do is to look for an organization, rather than an individual. How about if we make a list of all the organizations that have anything to do with this case, likely or not!"

"Yes, Mel, why not? Do you want to do it now, or back at the hotel?"

"No time like the present, my darling, can we use your indispensible notebook?"

"Here we are. Oh, first let me transcribe the notes I made in Norman's office," said Alex, "you never know, they could be relevant to this organization thing. Let me see … Now, what's this? Oh I can see now."

He spent a few minutes writing the transcribed notes, on the facing page in his notebook, and then said, "Right, Mel, here we go! The first three or four are formal acknowledgments of invoices and so on, but this next one is more interesting for us – it's a pity really that we only pinched the first page. This is roughly what it says – it's addressed to Sidney Poole, Director, Moorlands Engineering. Now there's a familiar name! *'Dear Mr Poole, after an exhaustive search of our accounts, I have been unable to find any reference to your invoice No. 13468, dated 4th July of this year. We do have your Nos. 13445 and 14002, of the 14th May and 11th August, respectively, which are both marked complete, with our rubber stamp.'* Then it runs out and presumably continues on the next page."

"Interesting because of the addressee, yes," commented Melpomene, "but it doesn't tell us any more than that there was business going on between Moorlands and Gormsby's. Any more?"

"Nothing, nothing, nothing – ah, what about this? Letter to Head Office, Winstanley Holdings: Attn. Mr R.B. Phillips, Chief Accountant. It says, *'As I think our Mr Felton has brought to your attention on a previous occasion, we are receiving several invoices a month from Moorlands Engineering in respect of services or goods we do not purchase from that firm, for example, farm tractor tillage appliances. Mr Felton has instructed our accounts receivable officer to return these marked 'incorrect' to sender, but they still continue. They appear all to be sent over the authorising signature of a Mr Blanche or Blanc. We would welcome your instructions in this matter.'* What on earth is this all about?"

"Alex, would there be any point in contacting those auditors who went through Moorland's books with a fine tooth-comb over the embezzlement? There could be material not relevant to the trial that was never brought out, couldn't there?"

"Maybe, Mel, but the trouble with that is that auditors are usually obsessed with confidentiality. We would need a court order or similar, or the authority of the Moorlands board before they would release anything. Good thought, but perhaps to be held in reserve. And it doesn't seem that I was able to snaffle anything else of interest from that file. So are we going to start making a list of organizations now?"

"Right let's. Starting locally, we have the hotel, the police force, the court system, then the Andover prison and, of course, Gormsby's mill," said Melpomene, "and I suppose we should include the Green Man pub."

"Is a pub an organization, then?" asked Alex, to which Melpomene replied, "As far as social anthropology goes, certainly – and it contains subsidiary organizations, such as the staff, the denizens of the public bar, and so on. And to break it down further, the public has its regular drinkers, the darts fraternity, and outsiders, such as charabanc trippers. I don't suppose we shall find ourselves analysing these to any depth, but it's useful to start off with a comprehensive list!"

"I'm beginning to see," said Alex, "and now, I suppose we can extend the scope to our little society at Crabbe and Crabbe, then Greene and Jerrold, and on and on!"

They spent the next hour refining their list, while the Tessie's waitress brought, first dessert – Mel had apple crumble and ice-cream, while Alex opted for Stilton and crackers – and then a succession of cups of coffee.

At last, Melpomene suggested that they had a good basis already, and that they might be better sleeping on it. "When we look at our list next, we shall probably see things in a different light, put each of the organizations in a separate balloon, and then we can start drawing lines within and between them. You'll see how it works, Alex, and how it suggests new leads to be followed up."

"I'm very impressed, Mel, I've heard you talking about your social anthropology, but I didn't realise it was so scientific! I am really impressed, my dear!"

"And this is only one of the many approaches, you know – the people who deal with tribal societies have a somewhat different take to this one. We live in an industrialized society, so that ancestors, descendants, aunts, cousins and so on are, most of the time, not thought of as being very important, while employers, workers, clients and customers are what we deal with predominantly."

They paid their bill and left a big tip for the waitress, Melpomene saying, "Thank you for not disturbing us while we were working! Lovely meal, we shall come again!"

On the way back to the hotel, Melpomene spotted a stationer's, where she bought a big roll of cartridge paper and a selection of coloured pencils. "We shall have fun with these tomorrow, Alex, but meanwhile we should do something else to clear our heads. How about a couple of games of two-handed cribbage?"

Chapter 21

At dinner, which reached the hotel's usual high standard, the Aunts asked Melpomene whether she and Alex would join them for bridge afterwards. "Not this evening, I'm afraid – Alex and I are working on a case. You'll hear all about it in the fullness of time, I promise you!"

In their suite, Mel unrolled the cartridge paper and cut it into sheets that would fit the table in the sitting room. It needed holding down at the corners to stop it curling, so she found several small pewter ornaments that were heavy enough.

"Now, Alex, let's look at the list and decide the best way of setting the organizations out. I've only done this sort of thing two or three times before, as exercises during a new course on Sociometrics at LSE – and they were probably set up to be easy beforehand – so we should be prepared for a false start or two. To begin with, it seems sensible to put Gormsby's in the middle – after all, it's what started everything!"

They spent the next couple of hours happily drawing squares and circles with various coloured pencils, and joining people to others with whom they were related with lines of different weights, single, double or dotted. It was quite late before they decided to finish for the day, had cups of hot chocolate and biscuits brought to the room, bathed and went to bed.

In the morning, before they went down to breakfast, Alex called the chambermaid and asked her not to tidy up any of the 'mess' on the table or even on the floor nearby.

By mid-morning, they were beginning to come up with promising results based on their charts. As Melpomene pointed out, "We've got at least two places where there is a weak and spidery relationship showing up. First, it looks as though we shall have to find out more about the connections between Gormsby's, Moorlands and Winstanley Holdings – and I'm puzzled how dear Mr Blanch fits in to this, if at all. Then, of course, there are the villains – Jerrold, Greene and the charming Osgood. We've already got David Wilkinson pursuing enquiries for us – let's find out whether he has heard from Detective-Sergeant Manley in town."

"Yes, Mel, I agree – but I think that this time it would be good to go and see him face-to-face at the police station – by now he might have some written reports for us to look at. We'd better ring first, to make sure he's available to talk to us – it's possible that he has other police business on the go, as well as ours, you know! And while I'm about it, I'll ring Marjorie too, to see if she has anything new. Can you check us out while I do that?"

After making the calls, Alex said, "Right, Mel, off we go! Wilkinson says he's got some interesting stuff for us. I told Marjorie we would be home later today, and asked her to ring the flat and tell Mrs Mountain and Caroline, so they could get some supplies in. It's only a local call for her – goodness knows what our telephone bill will be here after all the toll calls!"

At the police station they were shown into the superintendent's office and welcomed warmly by David Wilkinson, who sat them down and pointed to a stack of papers on his desk, saying, "Most of those are for you, but before we start going through them I'll tell you that at last an arrest warrant has been issued for Vincent McKinley Greene. The only problem will be finding him – he has gone to earth! DS Manley and his boys have been scouring all the likely places, including his office and his home – apparently he lives in a boarding house in Spitalfields, and so does Jerrold, would you believe! Hardly the place one would expect to find respectable lawyers – but, then, we know that neither of them is respectable! I've told Jimmy Manley to hold off till he's spoken to you two, so that you won't muddy each other's tracks too much."

Melpomene said, "That's sensible, David, thanks. We've been working out a few connections, so that might give us fresh ideas for the hunt. Now, what else have you got for us?"

"Right. First, here is a list of all the chemists' shops in Woodhampton, with the entries from their poisons books. It appears that there were only four sales of nicotine in the town over the last six months. Two of them were to well-known nurserymen around the district – apparently it is used in horticulture – and one to your Mama's head gardener! We shall eliminate those for the moment, I think, but we may need to interrogate Lady Musgrave under blinding lights later on! The other entry had a name on it that we cannot verify – the person who sold it says he was shown a driving licence as the identification that is required for poison sales, but that name does not appear on the licence files, the local Kelly's or the telephone directories. Maybe he wrote it down wrongly, who can tell! Someone who bought nicotine with evil intent would give a false name in any case."

"That is a good approach," said Alex, "we could do similar searches in the districts where Greene lives and has his office. But he could have bought the stuff anywhere."

"Or maybe his gang has stocks of a range of useful drugs!" added Melpomene, with a grin, "What's next, David?"

"DS Manley investigated the Greenwich address corresponding to one of the cars you spotted at the Mill, Mel. His report, here, is quite long, so you had better take it with you to study at leisure. Are you going back to town, today? Manley is at Mile End Road police station – I know he is looking forward to meeting you both. He said that Alex, as a lawyer, would probably be more successful with enquiries about Jerrold, at the chambers he shares at Gray's Inn, than he would as a policeman, so he's left that task for you."

"And finally, I asked my contact at Criminal Records whether they recorded aliases used by contacts, and, if so, whether he could find any 'Osgoods'. He came up with two that might match your physical description, and one villain actually called 'Osgood' – but that was a woman with repeat prostitution offences, and she is small and slim, besides. Copies of the two entries are in this file, too."

"My word, David," said Melpomene, "not only shall I put you in my will, but I shall dedicate my next paper for the Journal of Social Anthropology to you! Thank you very much!"

All three went along to the station canteen and drank mugs of tea, that, as Mel commented, "You could stand the spoon up in!" accompanied by scones and butter obviously designed to sustain policemen over an eight-hour shift.

Then they got back into the Alvis, stowing the files along with the latest charts in the dicky-seat, where they would be safe from blowing away, and set off to London, Melpomene driving, with her fair curls confined under her backwards cap.

A couple of hours saw them at their flat. They parked the car in its usual spot in the mews and climbed their stairs, to be welcomed by Caroline, the housemaid, and Mrs Mountain, the housekeeper – whom they would never think of addressing by her first name, even if they knew it, which they did not.

Chapter 22

"Nice to see you both again!" said Melpomene, "I hope you had a more relaxing break than we did – but I wouldn't want to change anything, really! We shall be in for dinner, with any luck, Mrs. M – we shall leave it to you what you present us with! And Caroline – has there been any interesting-looking post – I can bear to wait a while before we attend to the bills!"

"Well, I don't know, ma'am, what you might call interesting," said Caroline, "but there's one from Yorkshire, I noticed. Here they all are. I kept them in the drawer of the hallstand for you. Cups of tea?"

"Oh yes, thank you, and Mr Alex would like one I'm sure!"

"Yes, please," said Alex, "but I must first make a couple of telephone calls – I noticed the phone bill among the letters, but I won't open it yet!"

When he had finished phoning, Alex joined Melpomene in the lounge, where she had been going through the letters. "I rang DS Manley at Mile End Road first, Mel. He'll be at the station until about six, so I said we'd come and see him before then – we must go through his reports first. I also rang the local Post Office and asked whether they keep copies of Kelly's street directory. They say they have all the London ones, and some for the closer towns in the Home Counties. I thought that tomorrow we might look around the Greenwich address that turned up with that car number, and also poke around Greene and Jerrold's boarding house in salubrious Spitalfields. They obviously haven't chosen such a place simply for the views of the landscape, nor for its historical connections with Jack the Ripper! Anything in the post?"

"That Yorkshire letter that Caroline spotted was from Sir Ansett Browne, at Winstanley Holdings," replied Melpomene, "he says that he was told by Norman Felton that if he had any sensitive information to pass on, he should contact us, because we could be relied on to keep it confidential. Norman asked my Mama for our address – she only knows this one, not the office. And then Sir Ansett goes on – I'll read it to you, Alex: *'You may or may not have already guessed that I am being forced into certain actions against my will and better judgment. I am ashamed to admit that this pressure is being exerted on me by a fellow director, and that heretofore I have been too cowardly to resist it. My only excuse is that this person is in possession of information that, if disclosed, would likely bring about the downfall of my business reputation, and with it my fortune and the support of my family. I would like to meet with both of you, to explain further and to ask you for help, but I have come to realize that my every movement is being watched. Mr Felton has assured me that you are both resourceful and brilliant, and so I propose a stratagem that I am confident you will be able to accept and pursue. It is this: my wife and I are opera lovers, and we have a reserved box at Covent Garden for the whole season. We hope to attend the evening performance of Tannhäuser the Saturday after next. If you present the enclosed note at the box office, you will be given two seats in the circle, close to the private boxes. We often have friends drop in during the intervals, so you will hardly be noticed if you come to our box, No 4, during the intermission that follows Act One. Please do not respond to this letter, as all our letters and telephone calls are being checked. I will post this surreptitiously in a street pillarbox at night, as I take our beagle dog for his walk. Please help! Ansett Browne.'* How about that, Alex?"

"Amazing stuff, my dear! It almost gives me the impression that we are becoming *bona fide* detectives! What do you say, Mel, do we go along with this?"

"How can you possibly doubt it? Is your dinner jacket clean and in good condition – no soup stains? I think that this justifies my purchase of a new glamorous evening dress, and having my hair done, don't you think, Alex? Meanwhile, back down to earth – are you ready for a trip to see Detective Sergeant Manley? The Underground, I think, according to the map it looks like there's only a short walk at the other end."

Melpomene shuffled the remainder of the post without coming up with anything more interesting than an offer to Alex of a concessionary subscription to 'The Fortnightly Review', together with a free sample of the current issue. She riffled the pages, but nothing appealed.

"Have you got the report from DS Manley about the Greenwich address, Alex? We ought to see what he has found before we set off. Thanks, let's see, now: *'Investigation centred on: Feather, J.E., 27 Fillmore Gardens, Greenwich, SE 10. This address is a modest semi-detached house, well kept up, no garage, well-tended front yard with patch of grass and flowerbeds. On ringing doorbell, woman appeared, saying that she would have nothing to do with door-to-door salesmen. DC Thompson showed his warrant card and asked to see*

Mr Feather, whereupon the woman said that he had been a lodger there once, but had not lived there for several months. She could not provide a forwarding address. When Thompson asked what sort of a man Feather was, she answered that he was no different to any other railway clerk, she supposed, but provided the information that he was possibly in his forties, unmarried, middle height, with a small moustache, and balding greying hair. She also said he was quiet enough at first, but had been looking very worried for a few days before he suddenly left, with two weeks' rent unpaid. When asked whether he drove a big Sunbeam car, she laughed and said he didn't seem well-off enough even to own a bicycle.' "

"Not much help, eh, Alex? Feather is not likely to be a principal in the affair, and it's probably not worthwhile to spend too much energy hunting him down – he won't know much and he will be intimidated as well – the woman said he was looking increasingly worried. I'm beginning to suspect they have a succession of expendable people who are used simply to conceal the real players. The car was registered in his name to protect the real owner, but it must be kept somewhere – I wonder whether DS Manley has organized a watch for it. He goes on to report how they made tentative enquiries in several neighbouring houses, with not much hope of finding anything further."

Alex nodded, and put on his hat, "To Mile End Road!" he said, stood aside and followed Melpomene down the stairs. There was one change of station en route, so it was nearly half an hour before they were asking for Detective Sergeant Manley at the desk of the police station. The desk sergeant rang through and DS Manley appeared down the stairs and welcomed them. He was youngish, with an impressive ginger moustache and hair to match. He took them up to his section, and introduced DC Thompson, a plump man, probably a few years older than Manley, who was working at a desk in the corner.

"We saw your report on 27 Filmore Gardens," said Alex, "did you manage to track down anything more?"

"No, but we're still working on the Sunbeam car, HF 1056. According to records, it will need renewal at the end of the month, so I've left a memo with the registration office to let us know when the renewal is presented – if it ever is, of course. When that happens, they're going to give the person registering some excuse for waiting, and get in touch with us. Depending on the office location, we'll send someone to interrogate them."

Chapter 23

DC Thompson continued, "We've also listed a description of the car with all stations in the Metropolitan area. It's a bit much to hope that it will be spotted, but it's worth a try. We did try knocking on a few doors in the neighbourhood, but in my experience this rarely brings any results, unless you have something specific to ask, and we didn't, really. It looks as though the houses in that street are all ordinary single-family dwellings. A few might take in lodgers like Feather, but in my opinion, we're barking up the wrong tree, here. Since the woman described him as a 'railway clerk', we tried inquiring at the closest railway stations, Greenwich, Maze Hill and Westcombe Park, but none of the station masters or their assistants had heard of any Mr Feather, nor did our description ring any bells with them. She could have just been guessing."

"Thank you very much, anyway," said Alex, "you've gone to a lot of trouble for us, for little reward." "That's perfectly all right," said Thompson, "anything that gets me onto my feet and away from the paperwork is welcome! Just kidding, Sergeant!"

"He's quite right," said Manley, "the public would be surprised to know just how much police investigation is done with files and documents! Forgetting Feather for the moment, let me tell you what we have been doing to try and track down Greene – I believe Superintendent Wilkinson said that Mr Crabbe intended to go to Gray's Inn himself to see whether he could find out anything about Jerrold, is that right?"

"Yes," said Alex, "being a solicitor myself, I thought that the clerks at his chambers would be more inclined to talk to me than to the police – it will not be news to you that relations between the two professions are not always comfortable! I am going to go there soon – but for now, what of my esteemed colleague, Mr Vincent McKinley Greene?"

"I phoned up my opposite number at Brick Lane, the police station that is closest to Weavers' Mansions, the boarding house where both Greene and Jerrold live, …"

Melpomene interrupted, "Did you say Weavers' Mansions – that's a bit of a coincidence, isn't it?"

"Not really, Mrs Crabbe, that whole area was once a refuge for Huguenot silk weavers, who had fled Europe during the purges, so I suppose that's where the name comes from. As I was saying, DC Webster, of Brick Lane, went and made enquiries at the boarding house, which seems respectable enough, though it is in a run-down neighbourhood. I have some notes here. He spoke to the manageress, a Mrs Pontefract, and she told him that, yes, the two were long-term tenants, but that she had not seen them for several days. She was used to this and thought they must be away at the assizes somewhere, or at some similar business. She said that they often worked together, as far as she knew. She added that there was another barrister, a Mr Holdsworthy, living on the same floor, and that all three sometimes went to the local pub together of an evening, 'But they always behave themselves!' she said. Apart from those gentlemen, most of the other tenants were clerks or shop assistants, occupations like that, mostly single men, except for a retired couple, Mr and Mrs Arnaud, French she thought, who lived on the ground floor back."

"That's very interesting, but unfortunately it doesn't advance us much, since they are away," said Alex, "maybe I'll get a chance to speak to this Holdsworthy some time – I wonder what chambers he uses. Did your oppo find out anything else on this occasion?"

"Well, only that he asked Mrs Pontefract what was the local they frequented, and she promptly replied, 'The White Rose, round the corner.' DC Webster didn't think there was much point in going there at that time, as it was early afternoon, and the regulars wouldn't be there then."

Said Melpomene, "We have some experience in public bars, haven't we, Alex? We might find it useful to go there at some time, but perhaps Alex should go to Jerrold's chambers, before we lose the thread. Thank you very much, Sergeant and Constable – I assume it will be all right to call on your services again?"

"Of course!" said Manley, "Do you feel like a cup of tea before you go? DC Thompson and I keep our own supplies of decent tea here in our office – station urn tea can get a bit stewed!"

"We're tempted!" said Melpomene, but we'll leave that pleasure for a later occasion! Back to the Underground – I assume, Alex, that you know the best station for Gray's Inn!"

"I always go to Chancery Lane," replied Alex, "because I know the way into the precincts of Gray's Inn from there."

Arriving at the Porter's Lodge, which reminded Melpomene of that at the LSE, Alex enquired whom he should approach to find out about the members, and was directed to the office of the Clerk of Chambers. This gentleman, a benign elderly man, invited them politely to sit down, and then asked their names and the reason for their enquiry.

He was visibly shocked to hear that Jerrold, KC, was associated with someone for whom an arrest warrant had been issued, but went on to explain that, apart from confirming that he was a member of Chambers and not currently in residence, he, the Clerk, could not possibly give them any information about Mr Jerrold without his permission or a court order to that effect, explaining, "As a solicitor yourself, Mr Crabbe, you must understand that there are stringent rules here. Such information might well be germane to court proceedings, might it not?"

"I quite understand," said Alex, "I apologize if I have given you any distress. Meanwhile, perhaps you could let me know whether a Mr Holdsworthy is a member of Chambers."

The Clerk said, "Yes, I know him, he is indeed a member," consulted an 'in/out' board on the wall, and announced, "and he is 'in' at the moment – would you like me to call him and see if he will see you?"

He lifted the telephone and made the call, then said, "He will have to leave for court in half an hour, but will see you now. You will find him in the building facing you across the walks, on staircase B – the names and floors are listed in the hallway."

Thanking him, Melpomene and Alex found their way to Holdsworthy's room, knocked and entered. The occupant, already attired in gown and wig, greeted them, saying, "Bernard Holdsworthy at your service – who do I have the honour of addressing?" Melpomene was surprised when Alex did not answer as expected, but seized the other's hand, saying, "Well, well, if it isn't Holdsworthy minor! Don't you remember me, Spider Crabbe, from school? May I introduce my wife, the Honourable Melpomene Crabbe, née Musgrave?"

There were hilarious reminiscences all round, which Mel had to break up, saying, "Down to business, you boys!"

Chapter 24

Holdsworthy looked at his watch, "Oh, is that the time! I had better get going – I'm supposed to be meeting my client and his solicitor outside Court No. 2 in ten minutes! If you don't mind walking with me, we can chat and you can tell me whatever it was that you came to see me for!"

As they set out, Melpomene said, "You know, these are my old stamping grounds, the LSE is only a step away from here! You two do your talking, and I'll look around nostalgically!"

They soon arrived at the Courts, and walked up the wide marble steps into the foyer, with its elaborately tiled floor. Holdsworthy said, "I must see my clients now, but it will not take me long to confer with them this time, and the main hearing will probably be postponed until tomorrow, given the hour. You will see a pleasant little coffee-shop in the Strand – out through that door and turn left – why don't I come and find you there once I'm free?"

Melpomene and Alex found the place easily and went in. It was obviously a favourite of the legal fraternity – there were barristers in wigs everywhere – but they found a table for two and ordered tea, and cheese on toast – they were both starting to feel peckish.

"So, Alex, did you get anywhere with Mr Holdsworthy?"asked Melpomene, "I was staring around, not really listening to your conversation."

"Actually, Mel, it was encouraging. I gave him a rough idea of our interest in Greene and Jerrold and asked him about his visits to the pub with them, and he said he only went with them because he was feeling a bit lonely. He normally lives with his wife and little daughter – in some suburb, I forget where – but they were having the house painted and the floors done, so his wife had taken the child back to Leicester to stay with her parents for a while. Jerrold, who has the next room to his at the chambers, heard that he was looking for temporary accommodation, and told him that there was a free room on his floor at Weavers' Mansions, so he took it. He started to say there was something that puzzled him about Jerrold and Greene, but that was just when we got to the Courts, so he said he would tell us more later."

A few minutes later, Holdsworthy appeared at the door and looked round for them, then came and sat down. "I fear that my client has little chance of success," he said with a sigh, "in these breach of promise cases the woman always has the psychological advantage – but we shall find out tomorrow – as I expected, the hearing has been postponed!"

"You were just saying that you were puzzled about our friends," said Alex, "can you give us an idea of what it was that made you think this way?"

"It was two or three evenings ago, I suppose," was the answer, "I walked from the boarding house to the pub with them – behind them, actually. They were discussing something in low tones, and I didn't want to appear nosy, so I held back a little. There is an alley just by the pub, and I noticed a largish car parked in it, facing out towards the street. Two things drew my attention – the first was that the driver appeared to be sitting on the wrong side! Then I woke up to the fact that it was an American car – a Packard, I think. Then the driver threw a glowing cigarette butt out of the window as I passed, and immediately lit up again – I could see the flare of a match, which revealed his face for a moment. He seemed to have a long drooping moustache, but it could have been just a trick of the light. Anyway, I thought no more about it, caught the others up and we all went into the saloon bar together. Once inside, we went to the bar and ordered drinks – they had beers and I felt like a scotch and soda – then we went and sat down on a banquette against the wall. As we were starting to talk – Greene was complaining about a client who he thought was trying to pull a fast one, as they say – two men pushed their way through the press and sat down at a table near by. When Jerrold saw them, he grabbed Greene by the arm hard – I saw him wince!"

"And then …?" said Melpomene, "Did those men spot this and react to it?"

"Yes, they certainly did! Jerrold and Greene started to rise to their feet to leave, but the bigger of the two – they were both tall and brawny – put his hand on Greene's chest and pushed him back down into his seat. Then the other one said to him, nodding in my direction, 'Ask yer friend ter leave quietly, we ain't got no business with 'im!' Greene just looked appealingly in my direction, and so I left – I used to box at University, but I somehow thought that the noble art would be of no value against these gentry!"

Melpomene was becoming more and more enthralled, "Did you see what happened next?"

"Well, not immediately! I left the pub quickly but quietly, crossed the road and stood in a deep shop doorway, opposite the alley with the Packard – I had a flash of clarity and took down the number of the car. The two thugs soon emerged, each of them holding one of the lawyers by the arm. I wouldn't swear that they didn't also have their hands on pistols! They hustled them to the car and pushed them into the rear seats. One of them stayed in the back – probably holding a gun on the captives – while the other joined the driver, who wheeled the car out of the alley and set off at high speed, switching the headlights on as they went! Is that exciting enough for you, Mrs Crabbe!"

"And for me!" said Alex, "You have done a wonderful job for us, Holdsworthy, let us repay you by treating you to a decent meal. What is a good restaurant near here – you must know them all! And tell me that car number now, and I'll put it in my notebook."

Holdsworthy, who admitted to Melpomene, with a grimace, that his first name was Clarence, recommended a superior restaurant within easy walking distance, and the three were soon sitting down enjoying a sumptuous meal accompanied by fine wines.

Alex felt obliged to fill Clarence in on many more details of the case, stressing that confidentiality was paramount, and then the two men returned to swapping school anecdotes, accompanied by much hilarity, until Melpomene threatened to dance the Charleston on the table to relieve her boredom.

This prompted Alex and Clarence, in turn, to invite her onto the floor to dance a succession of slow foxtrots, quicksteps, and even a tango or two, and the next hour or so was spent in that pleasant activity. They walked with Holdsworthy to the nearest Underground station, said farewell to him there, thanking him again, and then hailed a taxi to take them home.

Before they had a cup of hot chocolate and a bath, Melpomene idly flipped through some papers. She suddenly stopped, saying, "What a good job I looked, Alex! I just saw that the letter from Sir Ansett had taken several days to reach us – what he said was 'the Saturday after next' is really this coming Saturday! I'll have to get my new opera dress tomorrow!"

72

Chapter 25

The first thing Alex did after breakfast was to telephone DS Manley and let him know the latest developments. He was very interested, especially in the Packard car, "That's not a very common make in this country, especially ones with left-hand drive, so I'll get my informants on the job promptly – when did all this happen, two or three days ago? Oh, I suppose that was when their landlady noticed they were missing. Could you let me know Mr Holdsworthy's telephone number? I would like to talk to him and see whether he can recall anything further."

"You'll get him at Gray's Inn," said Alex, "I don't know whether he is still living at Weavers' Mansions – he might have gone back home by now. While we're talking, I'll tell you about our next possible bit of excitement – Melpomene and I are going to see Tannhäuser at Covent Garden on Saturday night – which will be a thrill for us, but is not really the main event!"

He went on to explain further, reading out Sir Ansett Brown's letter and saying that they intended to follow through as he had suggested.

Manley said, "I'm very glad you told me all this! If, as he thinks, your Sir Ansett is being watched by these villains all the time, perhaps we can set some watchers of our own to try and spot them. And this will also provide some security for you and Melpomene – I would hate to see you two grabbed and whisked away in your turn! I won't tell you any details even when I've set them in place – better that you don't know anything, then you won't send out unconscious signals."

Alex passed on much the same information, with Manley's reaction, to Superintendent Wilkinson, who chuckled and said, "As I thought, Jimmy Manley has his wits about him – you are in good hands there! By the way, Stephen Buckmaster and his companion lady magistrates sat at the Children's Court yesterday, and let both Tony and Sid Hoskins off with a caution, but warning them and their parents that they might not be treated as leniently again. And we are keeping our eyes on the kids in a limited way – when school starts up again in a few weeks, we will tell the teachers to watch out for strangers lurking around."

Melpomene was getting anxious to be off to the West End, "Will you come and help me pick out my new glamorous evening frock, Alex, or would that bore you excessively? And I need to get my hair done, I hope I can get an appointment at short notice."

"I shall beg to be excused this time, Mel, I have some plans of my own. I thought I might find out about purchasing a pistol! Just a small one, but something to make me feel a little more confident about tackling some of these new acquaintances of ours. According to the 1920 Firearms Act, I need to get approval from the Chief Constable of my area – with our police contacts, I should be able to obtain this without any problem, especially when I explain about our case – maybe I'll get onto David Wilkinson again and see whether he can suggest someone at the Yard to speak to first. I've fired revolvers in the Corps at school, so I won't need a lot of practice."

Melpomene was a little dubious, but saw that Alex had a point. "Go on, then!" she said, "Where will you go first, Scotland Yard? Will this take all day – in that case I'll see you here for dinner. I'll let Mrs M. know – about dinner, not the pistol! I shall head straight to Bond Street, of course."

"Good luck with your shopping!" said Alex, kissing her, bringing the reply, "You too, my darling, and be careful – I'll walk with you to the Underground."

At New Scotland Yard, Alex enquired where the gun licencing department could be found, and the desk inspector, after asking for more details, directed him to an office on the second floor of the main building, with a sign on the door saying "Firearms and Explosives Registry." Inside he found an office with several people waiting on benches. At the counter, he asked about the procedure, and was given a two-page form, "Fill this in, sir, please," said the clerk, "you will find there are spaces for two qualified referees, whose signatures must be obtained before we can process your application. Normally it will take four to six weeks to issue the Certificate, unless there are any hold-ups."

Alex was somewhat put out by this, and said, "Is there no provision for cases of urgency? I need a licence much sooner than that!" "Only in extreme circumstances, sir, and you would need to make an appointment to see the Superintendent in charge to discuss that. Would you like me to make enquiries for you now? I will need your full name and address, and some idea of the reason for urgency. Of course, if you are already dealing with a senior police officer, he might be able to assist you."

"Well, yes!" said Alex, "I know Superintendent David Wilkinson of Woodhampton Police well, and he is familiar with the circumstances of my case – would that be a help?" "I will endeavour to find out, sir. Please take a seat, and I will make some telephone calls. What is your name and the reason for haste? I will call you when I have found out."

Alex sat down, telling himself that there is never any getting over bureaucracy, and started to go over the notes in his book once again. Then he went over to the clerk and said, "Is it allowed to leave here for a moment, I would like to get a newspaper?" "Of course, sir!" said the clerk, "you will find that at the end of this floor, near the stairs, there is a tea-room, and they sell papers there. No hurry, sir! Have a cup of tea while you are there, if you like." and he gave a wry grin.

Alex took him at his word, and bought a cup of tea and a sticky bun. They only had the most popular papers, 'The Banner' and 'The Trumpet', so he bought a copy of the latter and sat down with it to enjoy his snack.

But there on the front page was a huge headline, 'Dockland Tragedy: Two Lawyers Drown in Car Accident!' He read on, *'This morning, as a gang of dockworkers at Royal Albert Dock were preparing to unload a ship of New Zealand lamb and were warping it in to tie up, one noticed what appeared to be the rear end of a car, complete with spare wheel, visible just below the surface, between the ship and the wharf. The alarm was raised, and workers managed to loop a wire hawser round the rear wheel and haul the car out of the dock by crane. It was then discovered that there were three drowned men inside, including one in the driver's seat. Police took charge and a search revealed that two of the passengers still had papers in their pockets, which enabled them to be identified as a Mr McGerald, a barrister, and Mr Green, a solicitor. The driver has so far not been identified. The police have so far released no further details. Our reporter spoke to the ganger involved, who made the following comments, 'What I reckon is that the car was trying to make its way along the dockside in the early hours, when there ain't a lot of light. He's obviously not seen the edge of the dock and driven into the water. I've seen this happen with drays and handcarts, but never a car – heaven help them poor souls – they wouldn't of stood a chance.''*

Chapter 26

Folding up the newspaper, and stuffing it into his side pocket, Alex quickly returned to the registration office. As he entered, the desk clerk beckoned him over, saying in a respectful tone, "Mr Crabbe, you must have some influence in high places! If you would please go to the supervisor's office, directly across the corridor, they will see to you there."

As he entered the office, a young woman stood up from her typewriter and said, "Mr Crabbe? Mr Greensleeves will see you now." She led him to a door, knocked and ushered him in. Behind a large mahogany desk was a heavy-jowled, silver-haired man, who waved him to a seat, saying, "William Greensleeves – I have the doubtful honour of being supervisor of firearms for the Metropolitan area. I'm not sure of their reasons – they don't tell me everything – but my superiors have decreed that in this special instance, you shall be issued immediately with a licence for a concealed pistol. Please sign here ... and here ... . This card, which forms part of your licence, is what you must present to the gun shop or dealer where you purchase your weapon and ammunition. I am obliged to caution you that any use of the weapon that results in injury or death will set in train an official enquiry. The best of luck, and please be careful, Mr Crabbe!"

He came round the desk and shook hands, and gave a slight bow as Alex turned and left. On his way back home in the Underground, Alex racked his brains wondering what the special circumstances might be that had prompted the surprising decision, then suddenly realised he had completely forgotten about actually buying a weapon! He glanced at the station diagram on the space above the carriage windows and saw that he was coming up to Tottenham Court Road station, in an area where he might well find a selection of gun shops.

The first establishment he tried in Tottenham Court Road turned out to be presided over by a rather superior gentleman, who smiled patronizingly and said, "Oh not pistols, sir – we deal exclusively in shotguns for gentlemen who shoot game! I believe that you will find places that handle pistols a little further down the road, or in the side-streets!"

Resisting the temptation to make a smart remark, Alex left, and soon spotted a small shop on a corner, whose heavily barred window was filled with target rifles, airguns and what looked like service revolvers. After twenty minutes of conversation, the proprietor, who seemed to know what he was talking about, produced an automatic pistol, which he called a Luger. "If you are accustomed to a revolver," he said, "I would advise you to try a few rounds on a range or somewhere private, as the automatic action of this one takes a bit of getting used to. I can sell you a shoulder holster, which can alternatively be clipped to your belt, or you can carry the pistol in a side pocket. Either way, you should work out a way of drawing it quickly when it is needed."

Alex decided to take it and fifty rounds of ammunition, paid and completed the paperwork. He asked the proprietor to show him how to put on the shoulder holster, and decided that this would be the way he would take it home.

Leaving the Underground station nearest home, Alex saw a newsboy holding a poster: 'Dockland Tragedy: Doctor Says Murder', so he bought a copy of afternoon edition of 'The Banner' and tucked it under his arm, since he didn't think he could manage to read it while carrying a parcel of ammunition.

He was soon at the flat, to find that Melpomene had beaten him home. "Did you see this?" he asked, brandishing the front page of the paper with its headline. "No, and anyway I rarely read those sensational stories!"

"Well, my darling, take your time and peruse this, it may well interest you. In fact, read it out to me, please!"

Looking a little puzzled, Mel took the paper, sat on a settee and started to read, in a rather exaggerated and theatrical manner, *'Dockland Tragedy: Doctor Says Murder. After a preliminary post-mortem examination of the three corpses taken from the Sunbeam car in the Royal Albert Dock early today, the doctor who had been called to the scene, Dr Arnold Robinson, whose practice is in the district, revealed to our reporter that in his considered opinion their deaths were not accidental, saying that all three were undoubtedly unconscious before the car hit the water. Their lungs were almost clear of water, whereas the natural tendency on sudden immersion in water is for gasping breaths to be taken. On further examination of the bodies, he had noticed a rosiness in the skin, which he said is often seen in cases of coal-gas asphyxiation. Further tests will be needed to confirm this. We also understand that the names reported in our earlier edition contain an error: McGerald's name should have been reported as Jerrold. The other lawyer is indeed named Greene, as reported, while the identity of the driver is still unknown.'*

Melpomene looked astounded, and started to read the story again, quietly to herself. When she had finished she said, "Of course, this does not solve our case at all, but it does eliminate some of the characters. I wonder whether this will have made the BBC news broadcast – we shall have to wait for an hour to find out. Let's have some tea – all this excitement, after the labour of having a perm and buying a dress has left me parched!"

She rang for Caroline and said, "China tea, please, my dear – and have you any little somethings we could nibble?"

"Yes indeed, madam, Mrs M was baking all morning – her blackcurrant jam tarts look and taste particularly good today!"

"Are you going to show me your new dress, Mel?" said Alex. "I'll show it to you, but I won't model it – you'll have to wait until tomorrow for that delight!" said Melpomene, and she carefully opened the box, removed the tissue paper and held the dress up. "I always like dark green velvet!" she said, "It seems to set off my fair hair nicely."

"Very fetching, my dear! And now I'll show you my purchase!"

He stood up, turned his back, and then swung round with the Luger in hand, being careful not to point it at her. "Look, I've got a shoulder holster, too, just like an American private eye!"

"Or an American gangster!" Melpomene said drily, "Are you sure you are safe with that thing?"

"I'm certainly not going to go brandishing it around unnecessarily! I would just like to feel the weight of it when we are anywhere in peril from thugs. Oh, it's getting close to news time, switch the wireless on, please, Mel."

The BBC news did not run the dockland story as its leading item, but later on it repeated much of what Alex and Mel had already read, but with one additional item: *'The driver of the fatal car has been identified, through fingerprint records, we understand, as Samuel Osgood Perkins, a habitual criminal with several convictions for violent crimes. The next of kin of all three have been informed.'*

"Well, well!" Said Melpomene and Alex, almost in unison!

Chapter 27

Melpomene had a thought, "I wonder if anyone is keeping Norman Felton informed about all these happenings. I think I will ring him in the morning and put him in the picture, if he is not already in it."

"Good idea!" said Alex, "And then I want to talk to Jimmy Manley about our excursion to the Opera, too. He should also be made aware that I'm now a gun-totin' hombre!"

"I hope you are taking this gun business seriously, Alex! It sounds a bit like boys' cowboys and Indians games to me!" said Melpomene, "Or are you just feeling nervous about it? I am myself, a bit, I must confess!"

Mrs Mountain put her head around the door, "I can serve dinner whenever you're ready – it's rack of lamb, so I hope you've got good appetites today! And I've made plum duff for afters!"

"Sounds as though a bottle of red would be appropriate to go with that, Mrs M." said Melpomene, "What have we got in our extensive cellar?"

"Not a lot, madam, but there's one bottle left of that Coat de Roan what you brought back from France last year – shall I open that so's it can breathe?"

"By all means, Mrs M, that sounds perfect!"

After dinner, which indeed was delicious, if filling, both of them felt like relaxing for a change, so Melpomene settled down on a settee with her feet up, to immerse herself unashamedly in an Ethel M Dell book from the local lending library, which she thought had an appropriate title: 'The Swindler and Other Stories.'

Alex, on the other hand, decided to try something that he knew was almost a passion with Melpomene, and set out to attempt the lower slopes of the Times crossword, with a large india-rubber ready at hand. Neither of them went to bed very late.

On the telephone next morning, Norman Felton was enthralled by what Melpomene had to tell him – he had noticed, in passing, a story in the press about the dockland incident, but had not bothered to read it, as the Woodhampton paper had not made much of it.

"I shall not shed bitter tears over their demise!" he told her, "Especially on behalf of that Osgood – he got his just deserts, I would say! And the two lawyers will not be missed, either, but I hope their families, if any, are not suffering. What is beginning to worry me more and more is the growing evidence that the villains behind this plotting are ruthless and resourceful! Please let me know as soon as you can what you discover at Covent Garden this evening. That is the sort of adventure that I would not enjoy, but I suppose for a couple of young detectives it is commonplace!"

Melpomene laughed, "Far from it, Norman! We are both rather apprehensive, but we have taken certain precautions, which we will tell you about, hopefully, when this is all over. Has anything happened with you that we should know about? Any more attempts at sabotage?"

"Well, I don't know, really! You may find this a strange statement, so I'd better explain why I'm not sure whether or not it's sabotage. Yesterday, one of the senior loom-setters, Agnes Surridge, stopped me as I was walking through the shed and told me they were getting a lot more breakages of warp threads than usual. She said that a few of the weavers were accusing her setters of not doing their jobs, so she checked up and couldn't see that there was anything out of the ordinary in the way they were set up. Then she said something that made me prick up my ears, 'I think it's the warp yarn – it doesn't feel right!' So I told her I would check up and went to talk with the warehouse overseer, Ben Wormald. He is the one who orders yarn from the spinners, warp and weft, the lot."

"We were shown the warehouse before, Norman," said Melpomene, "but we didn't need to know anything about it at that stage, so we didn't ask. Tell me – the yarn is brought in there, is it, and the finished cloth is sent out, is that right?"

"Yes, Mel, we use, as you might think, huge quantities of yarn, and it comes from the wool-spinners in Yorkshire in closed rail vans, already wound on spools, that we call 'cheeses' – because of their shape, I suppose. In the wagons, the cheeses are stacked on wooden stillages, flat platforms that is, so they can be moved into the shed in quantity. Then they are stacked along one side of the shed till they are taken to the looms."

"I follow, I think!" said Melpomene, "So what did Mr Wormald have to say?"

"Well I saw that my comments rang a bell with him. He grasped my arm and led me to the rail siding, where two vans were being unloaded. 'Come in here, Mr Felton', he said and helped me up into a wagon. He asked the men who were unloading to step out and shut the door on us. They looked puzzled, but they did it. He then said something strange, 'Breathe in hard, please, Mr Felton, and tell me if this smells right!'"

"And did you smell anything unusual, Norman?"

"Not at first, Mel, but then I thought I could smell something like vinegar, or sour cream or the like, so I told him that. He looked triumphant and took me to the next wagon, had us shut in and asked me to smell again. This time there was no such taint! Then he said, 'this lot is from Wainwrights – we've been getting most of our yarn from them for donkey's years – but the other consignment we looked at is from a new supplier, you can see their label on the stillage, they're called Fenster and Churchman, of Leeds. I reckon that yarn has been got at before it left their mill! We keep it locked up in the warehouse until it's taken into our shed – and anyway, the wagons are all sealed until my men open them up.' "

"So I asked Wormald why we had changed supplier, and he said that he had no control over that, the orders came down from the head office of Winstanley, in Huddersfield, but that he assumed that we in the mill office checked all this."

"And do you?" asked Melpomene. "Well, we do see the orders, of course, but we don't really check anything – we assume that if Huddersfield wants to change suppliers, they must have a good reason for it."

"One last question, Norman. Do you know if any other mills in the group get their yarn from this new supplier?"

"I don't know, but I can certainly find out! And I'll ring the managers at those mills. I know both of them well – but I'm getting a bit suspicious of Winstanley's head office, so I won't mention it to them!"

"Thanks, Norman, let us know what you discover. It looks as though we'll soon need to visit Huddersfield!"

Chapter 28

Melpomene rang off, saying, "Phew, that was a lot of information for one telephone call!" She proceeded to give Alex a summary, and he made copious notes, checking back with her on some of the details.

"I think you're right about Huddersfield, Mel! Depending on what we find out from Sir Ansett this evening, we'll might need to work out a way of organizing a trip up there that will not arouse the suspicions of the villains too much. Now I'll ring Jimmy Manley."

Alex told the Detective-Sergeant all about the gun registration and what he had bought. Jimmy approved of the shoulder holster, saying that it had the advantage of keeping the pistol accessible even from a sitting position. "If you want to practice, come to Mile End Road station this afternoon – we have set up a room in the basement with sandbags and you can let off a few rounds to feel what the kick of the Luger is like. It's not the same as a revolver, such as the Smith and Wesson, so you wouldn't want to be taken unawares if you ever need to use it in earnest – but I hope this doesn't happen!"

"I'll take you up on the practice offer, Jimmy – would in an hour's time be too soon? Can I bring Mel? – I think it would reassure her to see that I can handle a pistol."

After cups of tea and some of Mrs M's jam tarts, they got into the Alvis and found their way to the police station. The desk sergeant recognized them and said, "Go down those stairs, please, DS Manley is waiting for you – I think he is catching up on his own practicing – we senior officers are supposed to shoot a round or two periodically to keep up our authorization to use a side-arm."

At he foot of the stairs they could indeed hear the occasional shot. On a door was a sign, 'Firing practice: do not enter while red light is on'. Alex banged on the door, the light went out and they entered to see Jimmy Manley and a tall man with inspector's pips looking at each other's paper targets and bragging a little.

After being introduced, the inspector left, saying, "I can't enjoy myself like this all day – back to my reports!" and Jimmy asked to look over Alex's Luger.

"Very good – fully loaded, not cocked and the safety on – all as it should be when carried in earnest. You had better put these ear-muffs on, Melpomene! Stand behind the line, Alex, and prepare your pistol for firing. I've pinned a new target up for you. Check around, and fire when ready, say five rounds to start with."

Alex found that, as he had been warned, the Luger kicked up more than a service revolver, but it only took the five rounds to accustom himself to it and feel confident. "Good!" said Jimmy, "Now let me see you unload the chamber and take out the magazine. Very good! I'm happy to let you loose on the underworld now!"

Alex thanked the Detective-Sergeant, and turned to leave, when Melpomene took him by the sleeve and said, "Not so fast, Mr Crabbe, what about me? I should be ready to take over if you are knocked unconscious in a melée or something!"

"Of course, Mel! Could you oblige, please, Jimmy?"

Jimmy grinned and took Melpomene through all the procedures, from loading a magazine to being ready to fire, then said, "Point it at the ground, Mel, while I pin up a target for you."

Like Alex, Melpomene was surprised by the first kick, but then had no difficulty firing the rest of the magazine. She unloaded the gun, while Jimmy retrieved the target, compared it with Alex' and whistled, then said, "Look at this – the groups are both pretty tight, but, if anything, I would award Mel the trophy this time!"

"Just beginner's luck!" said Mel blithely, blushing to her hairline!

They thanked Jimmy for the lessons, then Alex asked him, "Do we need to know anything about your arrangements for this evening? We'll be coming by taxi, and arriving at the theatre about half an hour or forty minutes before the rise of curtain, because we have to pick up our tickets at the box-office."

"No," he replied, "I would rather you didn't know anything at all! If, for instance, I told you that one of my men would be watching the box-office – which is not the case, by the way – you wouldn't be able to stop yourself trying to pick him out, which would tip off any sinister watchers-on! No, just try to concentrate on the opera, and the atmosphere at Covent Garden – have you ever been there before? So, go ahead and enjoy yourselves – at least up to the first act intermission!"

They drove back home, forced themselves to have a light lunch, even though neither had much of an appetite, because of apprehensiveness about the evening, and started to prepare to go out. Caroline, of course, had pressed Alex' evening clothes and Melpomene's new dress, and checked their shoes, so all they had to do was have a bath and get dressed.

Alex put on his shoulder-holster and checked that it did not make an obvious bulge, loaded his Luger, and even slipped some extra shells into an inside pocket. There was time for a last cup of tea, and then, telling Caroline that she and Mrs Mountain should not wait up for them, they walked to the taxi rank at the corner and set off.

At the Royal Opera House there was a throng of taxis, chauffeur–driven private cars and pedestrians streaming from the Underground, some in elaborate evening clothes, some more modestly dressed, and young people, obviously students, lining up in the hope of student rush tickets for 'the gods'. Said Melpomene, "That was us, not that many years ago!"

They made their way to the booking office, presented Sir Ansett's note, and were given their tickets and told, "Up two flights, turn to your left and look for door 18 – any uniformed attendant will direct you. Here is a program – enjoy your evening!"

On the way to their seats, Melpomene noticed an attendant with a familiar-looking extravagant ginger moustache, but she avoided looking at him, not mentioning it to Alex until they were in their seats.

The orchestra was already in place and quietly playing a selection of excerpts from the opera. Then the house lights were dimmed, and a spotlight illuminated the conductor, who bowed, turned and raised his baton. He lowered it dramatically and the orchestra broke into the familiar opening bars of the overture to Tannhäuser. Melpomene hugged Alex' arm, forgot all the other drama and prepared to immerse herself in the music, while waiting impatiently for Lauritz Melchior to sing.

Chapter 29

All too soon, Act One was over, and the roar of enthusiastic applause was followed by a buzz of appreciative conversation and a stirring of people leaving their seats, many going to one or other of the bars. Melpomene and Alex quietly made their way to the private boxes. From where they had been sitting, near the end of the row, it had not been possible to see into them, so they followed a sign indicating 'Door 18: Boxes A to E'. Outside each box was a card with the box-holders' name, so they were soon able to find the one assigned to Sir Ansett and Lady Felicity Browne. Alex knocked and pushed the door open, letting Melpomene precede him.

Inside there were three couples, animatedly discussing the performance. Alex coughed discreetly and said "Sir Ansett and Lady Browne? I am Alex Crabbe, and this is my wife Melpomene – so kind of you to invite us here tonight!"

A tall gentleman with greying hair stood and moved forward, "I am Ansett – may I present my wife Felicity? It was good of you to join us!" The two other couples made their excuses and made to leave the box, one man saying, "We're headed for the bar – can we get them to send in drinks for you, Ansett?" "No, no, Hubert – you go and refresh yourselves, and Felicity will come with you – but listen out for the Act Two gong, won't you?"

Sir Ansett shook Alex' hand and bowed to Melpomene. Switching to a more serious demeanour, he sat facing them and said, "I didn't, of course, know until this moment whether you would be able to take me up on my suggestion to meet. I have been increasingly anxious about those who are threatening our enterprise, and there have been signs that they will move into a much more serious phase before long. At our last board meeting, a day ago, some correspondence was tabled from Norman Felton at Gormsby's, asking about the sources of yarn supplies, and this seemed to make at least two of the board very upset, even angry."

Melpomene asked, "Was this to do with changing the supplier of yarn from Wainwrights to – what was it – Fenster and something?"

"That's right – Fenster and Churchman. I made discreet enquiries with the Chamber of Commerce in Leeds, and found that those two board members who seemed agitated are also on the board of F and C. There's something underhand going on here, I'm sure!"

Melpomene nodded and continued "I spoke with Norman Felton by telephone, and he says there is evidence of tampering with the yarn from Fenster and Churchman. He was going to get in touch with his counterparts at your two other Huddersfield mills to find out if any such interference was also affecting them. We haven't yet determined what form this tampering is taking, but it seems to affect the quality and strength of the yarn."

Alex broke in, "I'm getting more and more confused! If your two rogue board members are simply trying to get their spinning mill preferred as a supplier, then any tampering would be a disadvantage to them, not a benefit. It's beginning to look as though there are a number of interlocking and opposing plots going on here! What do you think, Sir Ansett?"

"I'm terribly afraid you're right, Mr Crabbe. There is also the whole ghastly saga of the murdered weaver, followed by the disposal of his murderers – did you see in the press that the driver of the doomed car was called Osgood – this must have been the same man who imposed himself on my meeting with Felton at Gormsby's, wouldn't you think? I fear that those behind all this are much more powerful and organized than we have imagined. One's mind turns to the Italian Camorra, or the American mobs, who are the cherished subjects of the makers of sensational moving pictures! Is this mere fantasy – I dearly hope so!"

Alex went on, "So, Sir Ansett, how many members are there on your board, and how often does it meet? Are they all regular attenders, or do some only turn up when there is something of interest to them on the agenda? By the way, who is it that draws up the agenda?"

Sir Ansett thought hard, and doodled on the back of his program. "There are fifteen members all told, and a dozen are conscientious attenders – there is an honorarium for those who do so, but it is only a formality, it doesn't amount to much. Our company secretary, Wilfred Hutchinson, draws up the agenda, after consulting board members."

"Now," went on Alex, taking out his notebook, "give me a list of all of them who you can think of. Initials will do, the names will not mean much to us, I suppose. Include yourself, of course! Thanks, I have, let's see, fifteen, that must be all of them. Now, let's go through them one by one, giving us a very brief comment on each I'm going to write them down, so please keep them short."

He read out each set of initials in turn, and Sir Ansett said things like: 'I'd trust him with the keys to my house' – 'morose, but not intelligent enough to be a plotter' – 'a genial soul, already rolling in money' – 'hmm, I don't know!' – 'a new member, don't know anything about him' – 'one of the F and C pair' and so on.

When he had been through the whole list, Alex said, "I have put stars by some of these – could I ask you to take this page of my book and add the names of the starred ones; you can give it or send it back to me later. I presume that I will find the full addresses of each of them in your company Annual Report? Good, I can get a copy of that from the Companies Register, I assume."

Then, the muted tones of the gong could be heard, signalling that the second act was imminent. Sir Ansett got ready to welcome back his wife and other guests, saying, "You two are entirely welcome to stay in our box for the rest of the performance, you know, there are enough seats." Alex and Melpomene thanked him, but demurred, saying, "Maybe we'll pop in during the second intermission, if that's all right."

As they left the box to make their way back to their seats, they noticed an argument, even a scuffle, going on in the corridor, between two uniformed staff attendants and a thickset man in an ill-fitting dinner jacket. They kept their curiosity in check, averted their gaze and hurried past, but Melpomene could not resist the temptation to glance back, and saw that the attendants were bundling the man off down some stairs off a side corridor.

Back in their seats, they saw that the orchestra members were still tuning up and resuming their seats, waiting for the reappearance of the conductor and the raising of the curtain for Act Two. Melpomene read from the programme – "*Hall of the Wartburg. Elisabeth agrees to be present at a prize contest of song, and enters the hall.*"

Chapter 30

Alex and Melpomene dropped into the Brownes' box during the second intermission, finding that Sir Ansett and Lady Felicity were sitting there chatting with only one of the previous couples. They were welcomed and asked to sit down, and Ansett explained that the other lady had been recovering from a broken ankle and was suffering occasional bouts of pain, so that her husband had persuaded her to leave, apologizing profusely to the Brownes.

"May I introduce my cousins, Phillippa and Desmond Finchley – not the Finchley Finchleys, I should point out!" said Sir Ansett, with a smirk.

The man shook hands with Alex, saying, "Please forgive Ansett, he always makes that joke, and we hardly notice it any more! In fact, we are from Kent – I have a pharmacist's shop in Maidstone. May we know your names?"

Alex introduced Melpomene and himself, but made no mention of their detective work, simply describing Mel as a social anthropologist and himself as a solicitor. Phillippa Finchley wanted to know what social anthropology was, so Melpomene gave her customary explanation.

Conversation soon turned to the performance, with all three of the ladies becoming bright-eyed over the singing and acting of the male leads. Alex commented that he had heard that Act Three was reputed to be rather sombre, but that his remembrance of Elisabeth's performance would probably be sufficient to sustain him, bringing the laughing comment from Melpomene, "Yes, Alex, you are often sustained by thoughts of beauty!"

Looking at his watch, Sir Ansett, said, "I think we have time for a cheroot – will you join me outside, Alex? I know you are strictly a pipe man, Desmond!" In the corridor, he lit up, offered Alex a cigar, which he refused politely, and passed him the list of names. Then he said, "I have recalled one more thing which could be important – it is to do with the company secretary, Hutchinson." He then stopped abruptly, looked around, put his finger to his lips and said no more.

Alex glanced discreetly around, but he could see no place where an eavesdropper might have been concealed, so he was a little puzzled by Sir Ansett's behaviour, thinking that maybe he was getting overwhelmed by all the intrigue.

Nothing more of any substance was discussed until the third act gong sounded, and they rejoined the others. Act Three was certainly tragic, but the music was nevertheless thoroughly enjoyable.

Melpomene and Alex thanked the Brownes for their hospitality and Alex said, "We may well be in Huddersfield during the coming few days – may we look you up?"

"Oh, certainly, certainly!" said Felicity, "Our number is in the book! Any evening will be suitable, as long as we know beforehand!"

Since there were hordes of happy chattering people streaming out of the theatre, Alex and Melpomene saw that they would have to wait for ages to secure a taxi, so they decided instead to walk to the nearest Underground and go home that way. It was not particularly cold, but Mel still felt chilly enough to pull her wrap more closely about her bare shoulders. Alex chivalrously started to offer her his dinner jacket, but she stopped him, saying, "Would you really contemplate walking along with your shoulder holster displayed to all and sundry?"

There were several groups of people walking in the same direction, apparently heading for the Tube, too, one or two of them actually singing little snatches of the arias from the opera, with mixed success and laughing at their mistakes. And then Melpomene was attracted by the sound of footsteps close behind them, and peering back could see a shadowy figure keeping close in to the wall of the building they were passing.

"Don't look now, Alex," she muttered quietly, "it could be my imagination, but I think we're being followed!"

They put on a bit of speed, trying to catch up to a trio of budding opera singers ahead, and the follower did the same. Fortunately, they were coming to a brightly-lit main street, with crowds of late-night strollers, some of them who had obviously just been turned out of a pub at closing time, so they deliberately mixed with them. Glancing back, they could no longer see their pursuer, if pursuer he was, so Alex said,

"Maybe we've lost him for now, but he may have guessed we are headed for the Underground."

As they entered the Covent Garden station and bought their tickets, Alex said. "Two things to watch out for here, Melpomene! First, keep an eye out for the ghost of William Terris – he was an actor stabbed to death in 1897 outside a theatre near here by a disgruntled rival and is said to haunt this station! Second, be careful when we go down to the platforms – there are only lifts here, no escalators, so we should make sure we only get into a lift with plenty of other people."

As it happened, they survived both these hazards and boarded a train that was quite crowded, with standing room only, so they had to 'strap-hang'.

When they were nearing their station, Alex put his mouth close to Mel's ear – the train was very noisy – and said, "I haven't noticed anyone suspicious, but in case he's watching for us to get off, let's work our way to the door slowly, and when we arrive at the platform, leave it until the last minute before jumping off. It might not work but it's worth trying!"

There were not many people on the platform, but on looking round it was clear that they no longer had a shadow, so they strolled to the flat in a more tranquil state of mind.

"I could murder a cup of tea!" said Melpomene, as they climbed the stairs. Mrs M and Caroline had taken them at their word and gone to bed, but there was a loaded teapot, cups, and a plate of freshly baked rock cakes waiting for them on the kitchen table, together with an envelope propped up against the milk jug, addressed to Melpomene.

She opened it and found a note in Caroline's best school handwriting, which read, "Dear Madam, your mother telephoned and asked you to call back, but not until tomorrow if it's after 11 o'clock when you get home. C."

Melpomene read it out to Alex, who said, "Take her at her word, dear – it's well after her deadline. It's probably something that can wait, otherwise she wouldn't have said that – don't worry, Mel!"

"Oh, I always do, Alex, Mama never rings unless it is important, she still thinks of the telephone as being for emergencies only, and much prefers to write letters. All the same, I will wait until the morning! Where's my tea?"

Chapter 31

As soon as she awoke, Melpomene went into the kitchen, where Caroline was bustling about, "I'll ring my Mama now, Caroline – thanks for leaving me that note – and I'll have eggs and bacon and toast for breakfast, please – and coffee this time, because I need to wake up!"

She rang her mother, who told her that, at about eight o'clock the previous evening, two gentlemen had arrived at the hotel by taxi and asked for accommodation. Once they had been settled in, they asked if they might have something to eat, and were served ham sandwiches and coffee in their room. So far, this was not unusual behaviour, but then something rather bizarre happened. When the room waiter went to collect the plates and to ask whether they required anything further, he saw that one of the men appeared to be cleaning a gun. When the man noticed the waiter staring at him, he gesticulated angrily and shouted something in a foreign language. The waiter, Henry, immediately withdrew and told the night manager, Mr Benson, who telephoned the police straight away. But by the time a sergeant and a constable had arrived at the hotel they found the room empty. There were not many staff on duty, and nobody had seen the men leaving. The police sergeant made some telephone calls and assured them all that the grounds of the hotel would be searched and that officers would be patrolling inside as well. That was when Lady Musgrave had telephoned Melpomene.

She went on, "Soon after breakfast this morning, in fact, less than half an hour ago, Superintendent Wilkinson arrived to take charge, the dear man. He arranged for a complete search of the hotel, from the cellars to the attics, with our staff helping. This is still going on! I can't help but be concerned, of course, but I feel much happier with him and his men around!"

Melpomene asked her, "Do you want Alex and me to come down now?" "Oh, no, dear! I much prefer that you stay safely miles away!"

"Well, all right, Mama, as long as you feel safe! Is the waiter Henry around? Alex would like to ask him a few questions if he's available."

Alex took the phone and was soon talking to Henry, asking him for a description of the men and whether he could see what sort of gun it was, but he was rather vague on both. "Well, all I can say is it were a pistol, not a rifle or shotgun – to tell you the truth, Mr Crabbe, I were a bit shocked! But I can tell you one thing – after thinking about it, I can tell you that the gentleman with the gun shouted at me in French – he said 'alley-voo' and I know that's French, because my Uncle Ted were in the war and he used to say that to me and my brother when we were little and annoying him, and my Dad told me then it were French! He said it means 'bugger off', if you'll pardon the expression!"

Alex thanked Henry, and asked to speak to Lady Musgrave again; then he told her that Mel and he would be going to Yorkshire and that they would telephone her from their Huddersfield hotel to let her know they had got there safely and to see whether she had any more news about the intruders, "Mel wants a word, too! Here she is."

Melpomene said, "I forgot to tell you – we enjoyed the opera immensely! We have resolved to go again some time, in between seeing good movies, that is!"

She rang off, and Alex took the phone, saying that he would like to catch up with Jimmy Manley about the previous evening.

After they had finished their breakfast and were in their room getting ready to leave for the North, Alex told Melpomene what Manly had said – that the sinister figure following them to the Underground was in fact one of his men, "I shall have to give him a wigging about letting you notice him – but not everyone is alert as Melpomene, I must say!"

As for the scuffle outside Sir Ansett's box at the theatre, Manley confessed that again one of the attendants was a policeman – and that the fellow that they had grabbed was "merely an ordinary sneak-thief, looking for handbags left on seats, or jewelry that could be snatched from ladies' necks. West End theatres are often a haunt for these opportunists!"

Alex said he had promised to let DS Manley know anything of interest to him that might come up on the Huddersfield trip, and returned to his packing.

He said, "We'd better get the car filled up and checked thoroughly before we set out – it would be frustrating to have any trouble on the road. I've been looking at the map, and we shall be on the A1 all the way to Leeds, where we'll branch off to Huddersfield, only about twenty miles, so we won't have to be constantly wondering about the route and instead can enjoy views of the countryside. It's not much more than 200 miles, so with any luck we can do it in four or five hours."

"But, don't forget lunch!" said Melpomene, "We can surely find somewhere nice on the way. And it sounds as though we'll have plenty of time to find ourselves a good hotel in Huddersfield – there shouldn't be much demand for rooms at this time, it's hardly a tourist area, is it?"

All went well, and, after a satisfying pub lunch in one of the small towns en route, the Alvis pulled up in the courtyard of 'The Weavers Arms' in Huddersfield soon after five o'clock. Melpomene had spotted the sign to this hotel and had not been willing to ignore its omen! Nevertheless, just in case, she sent Alex in to investigate. After a very short interval, he re-emerged, giving a 'thumbs-up' signal, and soon they were unpacking in a well-appointed suite on the first floor, even a telephone being provided!

There was a telephone directory as well, so Melpomene lost no time in looking up, 'Browne Sir A & F, Smedley Court, W. Hudsfd.' She made a note of the number, saying, "We'll telephone after dinner, but not too late. While I'm about it, I'll try another couple of numbers – how about 'Hutchinson, W', the company secretary?

She found the number – there was only one Hutchinson with that initial, and then, in a foolhardy moment, picked up the telephone and asked for it. When it was answered, by a woman, Melpomene put on a cockney accent and said, "Is Wilf there, dearie? Tell 'im it's 'is Auntie Aggie." She turned to Alex, with a mischievous grin and then an astounded expression crossed her face and she slammed down the receiver.

"What happened?" asked Alex, "you look as though you've seen a ghost! What did they say?"

Melpomene said, "Oh, Alex, I've nearly made a dreadful mistake! The man who answered said, 'For goodness' sake, Doris, you know you're supposed to start with the daily password. I'll overlook it this time, but if you do it again, I shall have to tell the Boss!' "

Chapter 32

Said Alex, "That was a salutary lesson, Mel! We must start taking this even more seriously than before, if that's possible. Trust nobody and suspect everybody! We have been assuming that some of Sir Ansett's colleagues and associates are in cahoots with the villains, so we should now take even more stringent precautions. Your experience just now has demonstrated without question that Wilfred Hutchinson, the company secretary, is in league with the devil. We have already started checking on the other members of the Winstanley Board, and I think we should be suspicious of the Brownes' domestic staff, too! We have no option but to trust the Brownes, themselves, of course."

"So, how should we cope with this, Alex?"

"I have an idea, Mel, but we will need to keep our wits about us all the time to carry it off. It's very likely that our names – Melpomene and Alex Crabbe – are known to some or all of the gang, so let's change them! I would be quite happy to be called, shall we say, Simon Tonkins. How about you? We should still be a married couple, we probably behave like one, even after such a brief experience of the marital state!"

"Very well, Simon, I shall be Daphne! Let me see – Daphne Tonkins, Daphne Tonkins, Daphne Tonkins! Yes, that sounds all right!"

Alex embraced her warmly, murmuring, "Oh, Daphne, Daphne, my love! – yes, I can live with that! Now, we should make sure that Sir Ansett and Felicity Browne are alerted to our new personalities. I hope that they can avoid letting our former names slip out!"

"Right, I shall start by getting the Tonkins invited to dinner soon. Listen to me, Simon, and warn me if I make any mistakes. Here we go!"

Daphne – formerly Melpomene – picked up the telephone and asked for the number.

A female voice, not Felicity, answered, so Daphne said, "May I speak to Lady Felicity, please? You may tell her that I am a recent acquaintance."

After a moment, Felicity answered, "Yes, who is this, please?"

"Well, this is really Melpomene Crabbe – we met at the Opera, and you were kind enough to say we could look you up once we were in Huddersfield – but we have decided that, for safety's sake, we shall stop using our true names in these problematic circumstances, Lady Felicity. I would like to be known from now on as Daphne Tonkins, and my husband as Simon Tonkins! I know this is a big imposition, but do you think you could try to keep to these names and forget the others? You will understand why, I'm sure."

There was silence for a few moments then Felicity answered, "Of course, Daphne! We are looking forward to seeing you and Simon! How about if you come to dinner here tomorrow evening, at about seven? I will, of course, tell Ansett about the new arrangements! It will be very nice to see you again!"

Daphne put the telephone down with a smile, and said to Simon, "This is a very intelligent woman, and equally quick on the uptake! I believe this will work out well, given any luck! I'll ring up Mama now and tell her we've arrived safely."

Daphne was soon speaking to Lady Cynthia, "Hello Mama dearest, we had a good run to Huddersfield and we've found a decent hotel, 'The Weavers' Arms' – we shall see how good their dinners are shortly. If you telephone us here the number is – let me see," she read it from the instrument, "but there is a slight complication! We are registered under our own names, but we have decided to use aliases otherwise, so that the forces of evil are put off the scent. This means that if you telephone and I answer 'Daphne Tonkins', you will know who it is – likewise with my husband Simon! Please tell David Wilkinson this, too. How is the hunt for the two suspicious characters going? Ah well, I hope they don't pop up again – maybe they've got nothing to do with our case. Look after yourself, Mama, and we'll let you know if anything important happens. Bye-bye."

Simon said, "And now I'll phone Jimmy Manley, and put him in the picture, too. This is all beginning to get quite complicated, but I think it will be for the best!"

Not knowing what the clientele of the hotel was like, they decided not to bother dressing for dinner, so after a quick wash and freshen up they wandered down to find the dining-room. There were not many there, as it was still quite early in the

95

evening, but Daphne was feeling ravenous, so they proceeded to order freely from the menu, which was an intriguing selection of unpretentious north-country fare, with some dishes bearing French names. They decided it would be safest to stick to the English items, and were not disappointed by them, nor by the burgundy that went along with them.

On the suggestion of their waiter, they went to a large lounge where there was already a log fire burning, and had coffee and liqueurs, while they watched the other residents and visitors, some of them playing cards or draughts, and others just chatting and drinking.

They were just discussing whether it was time for bed, when a minor altercation broke out near the doorway. A beefy man, in country tweeds, was arguing with a meek-looking woman, apparently his wife, "Nay!" he was saying, "I've had nobbut a couple o' pints so far, if tha wants to go 'oom by thysen, tha's welcome, but I'm stayin!"

A waiter or barman took his sleeve, in an apparent attempt to calm him down, but he was shaken off angrily, "Leave me be!" said the man, "I've as much right to be here as high-and-mighty Wilfred Hutchinson, theer!" and he pointed to a table where two men were playing chess. They were obviously embarrassed, and pointedly looked anywhere but at the troublemaker.

By this time his wife was weeping, and being comforted by a stout woman from another table. Then two hefty men, obviously hotel employees, were finally able to persuade the man to leave, followed at a short distance by his wife, drying her eyes as she trotted after him.

Simon looked meaningfully at Daphne, and they unhurriedly left the lounge and took the stairs to their room. "I wonder which of the chess-players was Hutchinson," said Daphne, "neither of them looked anything like my idea of gangsters!"

"I hope you are being ironic!" said Simon, "It would be much easier for the forces of law and order if every criminal wore a label – 'embezzler', 'arsonist', 'poisoner' or 'pickpocket' – but I'm afraid that the ungodly, in general, are indistinguishable from decent citizens – by sight, at least!"

"So you mean we'll have to resort to our wits, do you, dear Simon?"

Chapter 33

"How shall we spend today, Mel... – oops – Daphne? We're not invited to the Brownes' until this evening, so we might as well turn the time to some profit. I thought we might find out whether the University of Huddersfield, being in a region famous for the wool trade, has a textiles department or the like – someone there might be able to tell us about chemical treatment of warp yarns. If that senior loom-setter at Gormsby's – Agnes Surridge was her name, wasn't it – could feel a difference in the yarn, and if it had somehow been weakened, there might be someone who could suggest what might have been happening."

"And Norman said he could smell something strange, too!" said Daphne. "Oh, Simon, another thing! I had a thought while I was dressing this morning, idly wondering whether I should change my style as well as my name, and then I realized that our dear little Alvis is rather conspicuous, is she not? If Melpomene and Alex have been seen driving her, by anyone on the dark side, it might make them start wondering, were they suddenly to spot a similar car driven by Daphne and Simon, don't you think?"

"Good thinking, Daph!" "Oh, Simon, that sounds like a reference to daffodils! Please stick to my full name, or I shall start calling you 'Sime' which is getting close to 'Slime'!"

"Sorry, Daphne my love! I think you have something there about the Alvis, but I believe we have a way out. I have been aware for a while that she is due for a thorough service, and now might be a good opportunity. Let me make some enquiries – I'll ask at reception."

He made a call, to the desk, asking. "Crabbe in room 120. You may be able to help us with two things. First, could you please find us a number for the textiles department at the University, if there is one? And, secondly, is there an Alvis dealer in town? Oh good, I'll hang on for a moment. Excellent, let me write those down." Out came the faithful notebook and Simon made some notes.

"Success on two fronts, Daphne! First, I will ring the University – it turns out that there is in fact a department called 'Chemistry and Technology for the Textile Industries'."

97

When Simon spoke to the main operator at the University, at first she said, "I'm sorry, Sir, it is the long vacation, you know, so there is hardly anyone about. I will try the department office for you, nevertheless. Please hold on. ... Oh, Dr Bullock, I didn't expect anyone to be there. ... I see, I will give the enquirer your direct number, thank you very much. ... You are in luck, Sir, apparently there is a vacation course going on, and I just caught the person in charge, Dr Kenneth Bullock – if you ring him straight away he will still be there." And she gave Simon the number.

A man answered Simon's call, and when he explained what he was interested in, said, "That's not my main line – I'm more interested in the equipment side of things. You should speak to my colleague, Dr Tessa McPherson – she is at home this week, but I don't think she'll mind an enquiry – she is very keen!"

Simon rang the number he gave and Dr McPherson indeed seemed keen, saying, in a quiet Scots accent, "Why do you not come round to my place later on this morning and we can talk over coffee – aye, by all means bring your wife! I live in a wee flat in the city centre." And she gave her address.

"That's very good, Daphne!" said Simon and explained what he had arranged. "What about the Alvis?" asked Daphne, "Can we fit that in today, too?"

"Let's speak to the people in reception on the way out – they will know where Dr McPherson's flat is, and I can ask them where that Alvis dealer is, too."

The Alvis dealer turned out to be close to the city centre, only walking distance from the flat, and it was easy to spot the large sign, 'Prestige Automobiles: Rolls-Royce, Daimler, and Crossley a speciality.' Simon drove onto the forecourt, where there were already an AC tourer and a Lanchester limousine waiting, and he and Daphne walked into the sales office, where a young man in a spotless white dustcoat greeted them, with, "Oh, I say, is that Alvis yours? What a beautiful little bus! Are there problems with her?"

"No, we just want a pretty complete going-over and tuning. How long would that take, if you could admit the patient now? Would I be able to hire a car while she is in?"

"Oh yes, Sir, if you could leave her until this time tomorrow that would be good. If we find out we need any spares we will have to get them sent over from the main agents in Leeds. Meanwhile, there is a Riley tourer you could have while the Alvis is in. It belongs to our manager, but he's running in a new Crossley at the moment, for the wife of one of our best customers. Come through to the back and I will show you. There we are, the little green one in the corner. If you would like to take it, I will get one of our people to bring it round the front for you."

"I see you handle American cars, too!" said Simon, "Isn't that a Packard at the back?" "Yes sir, but we're just storing it for a customer, we're not set up to work on American automobiles – too many differences, you see!"

"We'll take the Riley – that's alright with you, is it Daphne? But we won't collect it until this afternoon. Shall we leave the Alvis where it is?" "Oh, yes, Sir, just leave me the keys and I'll get it taken round to the service bays. I'm afraid I shall need a service order from you."

As they strolled toward the city centre and Dr McPherson's flat, Daphne said, "I couldn't see see the number of that Packard – it would be amazing if it were the very car that was used to spirit away Jerrold and Greene. Did you get its number from Holdsworthy?" "Of course – I have it my little book! But I couldn't make out the number of the one at the dealer's either."

"I hope you're transcribing everything in your book to somewhere safe, Simon – imagine how you'd feel if you lost it or had it swiped!"

After only a short while, they came to the flats where Dr McPherson lived, and rang one of the six or so labelled buttons by the front door. After a while, the door was opened by a woman wearing a long overall.

"Dr McPherson?" enquired Simon "Oh dear, no! I'm just the landlady! Come in do – you'll have to go up three flights of stairs! Is she expecting you?"

The stairs were quite steep, but they took them slowly, not wanting to be out of breath when they knocked on the door.

Dr McPherson turned out to be an attractive woman, probably in her thirties, with red hair put up in a bun. "I'm sorry I didn't come down myself," she said, "I was busy looking at some slides. I'm Tessa. You must be Daphne and Simon."

Chapter 34

Simon and Daphne had already discussed how much they should divulge to Dr McPherson, since they knew next to nothing about her. "Let me just put it to her in general terms," Daphne had said, "and nudge me if I look like treading on dangerous ground."

After they had all exchanged pleasantries, and Tessa had invited them to sit down, she said, "What I was doing when you rang the door-bell was examining some wool fibres under high power – would you like to see?"

Daphne peered into the microscope, fiddling with the focus until she got a clear image, then said, "Amazing – it looks a bit like the trunk of a palm-tree! Have a look, Simon!"

"Yes," said Tessa, "those little scales are what gives wool its valuable properties, like absorbency and flexibility – don't get me rhapsodizing about wool or I'll never stop! Now, you wanted to ask me something, did you?"

Daphne asked, "Are yarns treated with chemicals at any stage, to change their properties, I mean?"

Tessa laughed, "You would probably be surprised at all the processes wool goes through on its way from the sheep to you! But, if we are talking only about what happens after it has been spun into yarn, there are some chemical treatments, yes. Often it is passed through an alkali bath to soften it, and of course it sometimes has to be dyed, unless the final woven cloth is to be dyed in the piece or printed. Have you got anything specific in mind – I'm a scientist, remember, so I need to be particular!"

"Right!" said Daphne, "Let's get down to details. Suppose someone, an inspector in a mill, say, suspects that a batch of yarn has been 'got at' to weaken it – he thinks it 'feels different' and there appears to be a faint scent of something pungent around the spools, what would be your first thoughts, Tessa?"

She unhesitatingly replied, "Acetic, lactic or citric acid would be my first guesses! If any of these had been sprayed onto the yarn, even in dilute concentration, or if the cheeses had been plunged briefly into one or other of them, and allowed to dry, then there would be such an aroma."

"And what about the strength of the yarn?" "Oh, certainly, depending on the exposure, the yarn would be weakened to some degree – maybe enough to affect the 'handle' of the yarn and to seriously degrade the quality of the woven cloth. This might not show up immediately, but the yarn would be effectively ruined!"

Daphne said, "Thank you very much, Tessa! We're very glad we came to you! We can't say much more at the moment – it is possible that there will be litigation later. Would you be willing to be called as an expert witness if necessary?"

"No problem, so long as I am properly briefed at that time! Now, what about some coffee and girdle cakes with honey?"

"Yes, please!" said Daphne, "I've just thought of a couple more questions, if you don't mind. If I wanted to buy a supply of one or more of these substances, where would I go? And would any of them be routinely purchased by, say, a spinning mill?"

"How do you like your coffee? There's cream and sugar here, just help yourself. When I've bought lactic acid in the past, through my department, I've got it from Hughes and Patterson, in Leeds. They are suppliers of all sorts of chemicals for industry. I can't recall using citric or acetic acid lately, I would have to look back through the files. You would have to ask a spinning firm about what they buy on a regular basis – at a guess, they would have uses for lactic acid, too. Did your client say anything more about this pungent odour?"

"As far as I recall," said Simon, "He referred to sour cream or vinegar."

"I vote for lactic acid, then!" said Tessa, "Acetic obviously smells like vinegar, but it wouldn't make you think of sour cream at all."

"In what quantities would it be needed to cause serious havoc?" asked Simon, "And how is it sold, in bottles, or what?"

"Hughes and Patterson only sell wholesale to industry, in carboys. People selling on in smaller quantities would repackage it in bottles."

"What is a carboy?" asked Daphne, "and how big are they?"

"You've probably seen them without knowing their name – typically they are greenish glass, with wickerwork as protection from breakage. They can hold five gallons or more each. I haven't got any here, or I'd show you – I do all my serious experiments in the department. And as for how much you would need, I would say that a ten per cent solution would achieve the effect you were looking for after half an hour's immersion, if you were a saboteur – but that's only a guess, really."

When they had taken a second cup of coffee each – Daphne saying, "If you want good coffee, you can rely on a chemical technologist, obviously!" they took their leave.

"We'll let you know how our enquiries go!" said Simon, "Thank you very much, Tessa, I hope we meet again soon!"

"Let's go and pick up this Riley," said Daphne, "I'd like to have a bit of a trial drive well before we need to set out for the Brownes' this evening. We could go for a little sight-seeing trip around the town – but I have no real expectation of many beauty spots – but one never knows!"

The keen young salesman at 'Prestige Automobiles' was only too happy to demonstrate the special features of the Riley tourer, including the pre-selector gearbox, of which he was particularly proud. He explained that it took a bit of getting used to, so Daphne was glad she had decided on a practice period. Simon had once driven an Armstrong-Siddeley belonging to a friend at University College that had such a gear arrangement, and it was not long before they were both adept.

They took turns driving around the outskirts of the city, which was distinguished more by factories and mills than by stately manor houses or picturesque churches, but it was still enjoyable. And the little Riley proved to be a delight to drive, pre-selector and all.

It was a surprise to them both to realize how time was passing, so they headed back to the hotel to bathe and change for their dinner at the Brownes'. As they went into the lobby, the receptionist handed them an envelope, as well as a note that they read at once, which recorded that they had had four telephone calls while they were out, one from Lady Cynthia Musgrave and the rest from Detective-Sergeant Manley.

The envelope, from Sir Ansett, had been left for them by a messenger, and the note inside read, "Looking forward to seeing you this evening. I will have a quiet word with you before we go into dinner, on a matter of some urgency. A.B."

Chapter 35

"Ring your Mama first," said Simon, "she may be getting anxious." When Daphne spoke to her, she seemed quite composed, simply wanting to report on the latest developments in the case of the gun-carrying interlopers. After some personal chat, she went on to say, "David Wilkinson is being his usual helpful and reliable self. He had wide enquiries made, and discovered that two men answering to our description had called into the Post Office in the afternoon to send a telegram, and had enquired how they could get to this hotel. The clerk had a copy of the wire – these are always kept on file – and made a further copy for the police. When David saw it, he rang, asked whether I should be telephoning you later and requested me to pass on the contents of the wire, which, as usual, was somewhat cryptic. I will read it to you, and post you a copy in the morning, as well. It says (all in capital letters, of course):

LAURELHARDY, WOODHAMPTON

ATT: STODDART, FENSTERCHURCH, LEEDS.

TRACKING QUARRY PROBLEMLESS STOP OUTCOME FOLLOWS STOP AGREED RENDEZVOUS 48 HOURS

Does this mean anything to you, dear?"

"It begins to, Mama, and I'm sure that between us Simon and I will be able to make something more of it. Please thank David Wilkinson for us! Did he say he would be following this clue up, as well? Good!"

Daphne wrote it down, checked it back with her Mama, then rang off and turned to Simon, saying, "Let's put this aside for a moment, while you call Jimmy Manley and see what he wants."

But when he rang Mile End Road, he was told that Detective-Sergeant Manley had gone off duty. The person who answered the phone said he was not at liberty to tell them Manley's home number, which, in any case was ex-directory.

"Ah, well!" said Simon, "we shall just have to try again tomorrow. We'd better put on a spurt now or we'll be fashionably late for dinner – I wouldn't mind were it not for this private message that Sir Ansett mentions."

They found the way to the Browne residence with no difficulty, and drove up a gravel drive to the front door, where they were met by a flunky in livery, who handed Daphne up the steps, and said that he would make sure that the car was parked properly. Simon, however, insisted that it be left on the drive, where it was not causing any obstruction, telling the man that the Riley had an unusual gear arrangement.

Inside the front door they were met by a maid, who ushered them into a pleasant sitting room, asking them if they would like a sherry or an aperitif. Daphne said that dry sherries would be nice, and the maid curtseyed and went off.

Soon a waiter arrived with the drinks, closely followed by Sir Ansett, who kissed Daphne's hand and shook Simon's. Closing the door, he pulled up a chair to face their couch and leant forward confidentially.

"Felicity and I entertain rather often, with various combinations of guests. We are of course very happy to include you this time, but because of your special activities, I thought you ought to be aware that others of our guests could quite possibly be involved in some of these nefarious activities that we suspect are going on behind the scenes. The safest approach would be to avoid discussing any sensitive topics, but I fancied that to do this might deprive you of the opportunity to pursue your investigations. So what I shall do is provide you with a little background to each guest. How does that seem, from your professional viewpoint?"

"A very good starting point!" said Daphne, "apart from hampering our work, the studious avoidance of particular topics of conversation might run the risk of drawing attention to them! The tricky part might be to provide the other guests with our background, without letting slip that we are inquiring into the problems at Gormsby's – but I think that it could be done in a straightforward manner – what do you say, Simon?"

"I agree, Daphne – you are an amateur student of social anthropology, which you have shown yourself good at explaining – and I am a humble solicitor in practice in London – I can certainly relate some typical cases I have met, while maintaining the usual professional confidence – end of story. So, throw us to the wolves, Sir Ansett – have any of them shown glimpses of their fangs?"

"You shall be the judge of that! We have three other couples this evening – Phillippa and Desmond Finchley you have already met."

"Ah yes, – the 'not the Finchley Finchleys'!" said Simon, "But surely we were introduced to them as the Crabbes?"

"Yes, but don't worry!" said Sir Ansett, "I have mentioned you to them since that evening, and they couldn't remember your names at all – perhaps they didn't listen at the theatre – I think they had had a couple of drinks then. In any case, I have known them both for ages, they are relatives and they can't be involved – they visit these parts only rarely. Let's set them aside. The other two couples are local, and directly linked to my business. I have given you notes on both before."

Simon got out his little notebook at this point, saying, "Go on, Ansett."

"The second couple are elderly neighbours. Brigadier Arnold Winter retired from the army last year, from a senior post at the Ministry. He sits on the Winstanley board, but hardly ever has anything to say. His spouse, Hermione, is a very pleasant cultured woman, but unfortunately getting rather hard of hearing, and self-conscious of this, so if you have occasion to speak to her, please raise your voices discreetly."

"And then we have Antoinette and Michael Stoddart – Michael is on the board and also a manager of some sort at Fenster and Churchman's – I have known them only for a year or two. "

Daphne's eyes grew round, and she flashed a glance at Simon, making him nod slightly. As far as they could see, Sir Ansett had not noticed. He went on, "I have so far merely mentioned to most of them that we shall be entertaining friends from London this evening – I made no mention of Woodhampton or Gormsby's. Will you be happy to meet them all?"

"Of course, let us join them, by all means!" said Daphne, and Ansett rose and led the way to the dining room.

The others were already seated around the long table, sipping aperitifs and chattering.

Sir Ansett said, jovially. "Here are our remaining guests, Daphne and Simon Tonkins!" and he took them round the table introducing them, before showing them to their places, half way between himself at the head and Felicity at the foot.

Chapter 36

The meal turned out to be delicious, the wines were well chosen, and the conversation was stimulating, ranging from the opera – the Finchleys could not forbear to relate the entire plot of Tannhäuser to the Stoddarts and the Winters, who displayed or simulated polite appreciation – through music and the graphic arts to horse racing and tennis.

Daphne announced proudly that she and Simon had been given a ticket to see the Wimbledon women's final last year, when Suzanne Lenglen beat the English girl, Kitty McKane Godfree, in straight sets. But then the Finchleys trumped her, saying that they were at the entire championships this year and saw Miss Godfree defeat the American Helen Wills Moody in three sets. Not content with that, they then took turns in describing, almost game by game, the latest men's final, an all-French affair in which Jean Borotra took five sets to beat René Lacoste. After that, the subject of tennis seemed exhausted!

After the main course, just as the desserts, pastries and cheeses were being put out on the sideboard ready to be selected, a servant appeared at the door and whispered in Sir Ansett's ear. He stood up and said, "Excuse me, Stoddart, you are wanted on the telephone – please go with Harris and she will show you where we keep it."

The buzz of conversation continued as the door closed behind them, but it was only a few minutes later that it burst open, and Stoddart staggered back into the room, white, sweating and trembling. He managed to gasp out that he needed to leave, and his wife rose to her feet, alarmed and went to him. Sir Ansett said, "You can't possibly drive in that state, old man, I'll get my chauffeur, Pinson, to take you both home – would you like me to call your doctor to meet you there?"

"No, no thank you Ansett – that won't be necessary, Antoinette will look after me, and I think I shall recover before long. Good night, everyone, I'm sorry to mess up the party like this."

There was speculation among those remaining as to the cause for Stoddart's distress, ranging from a sudden family bereavement to a rather unkind suggestion from Phillippa Finchley that it was a call from his stockbroker to say he was wiped out.

Whatever the cause, it was clear that the happy atmosphere of the dinner had been spoiled, and one by one the guests made their farewells, to unnecessary apologies from Ansett and Felicity Browne.

Simon drove back to the hotel – they had discussed which one between them had drunk the least wine at dinner – and they were soon safely in their room, having ordered hot chocolate on the way up.

Daphne started the inevitable speculation by saying, "At least we have confirmed that Stoddart for one is a villain. It has become clear that it was he who sent the armed intruders to the hotel – but we still don't know who their intended victim was – it could have been one or both of us, or it could have been Norman Felton. Can you think of anyone else, Simon?"

"And what was all that telephone business about?" said Simon, "I don't go along with any of the ideas that were raised after dinner. But let's not worry about it all now, or we won't sleep a wink! Bath and bed are the order of the moment, wouldn't you say?"

They slept well and were wakened by a maid who drew the curtains and left a tray with tea things on the table, accompanied by the London morning paper.

Daphne lazily took the paper and leafed through it, sipping a cup of tea. Then she exclaimed and almost dropped the cup.

"Listen to this!" she said, "Once again some lurid headlines seem directed at us personally! It says:

'BODIES IN THE BARN: Sensational Discovery at Hampshire Farm! F. Parslow reporting. Yesterday afternoon, a young girl, Peggy Annette Stevens, 16, of Pagsley, Nr. Woodhampton, Hants, was walking her dog, Fergus, a highland terrier, when he became interested in an abandoned farm building they were passing. Miss Stevens said that he almost pulled her arm off in eagerness to investigate something in the barn. When they got inside, the dog dragged at some sacks covering a pile of something in the corner. Then, to her horror, she saw what appeared to be a body, so she picked up the dog and ran out. In the lane she met a farmhand, Mr Silas Brent, cycling home from work, who calmed her down and rode to a blue police telephone box and called the police. Later, a police spokesman, Inspector Wright, told this reporter that there was not one, but two bodies, and furthermore they had both been shot in the* *back of the head. One, identified by his passport as Bertrand Chausseur, a French national, was found to be wearing a shoulder holster, but there were no signs of any weapons on or near either of the corpses. The other deceased has not at this time been identified. Inspector Wright said that although the victims' cause of death was obvious, autopsies would still be required.'*

"Are you putting two and two together to make three, Simon, like me?" said Daphne, "Surely these two must be the ones who intruded into our hotel? I suppose the rendezvous mentioned in their telegram could have been the barn where they were found. I imagine that any of the hotel staff who saw them would be able to identify them, especially Henry, the room waiter. David Wilkinson will be on to this, I'm sure."

"And," said Simon, "this is a plausible explanation of Stoddart's behaviour last night! If his gang-land boss had found out that Stoddart's assassins had failed in their attempt, whoever their target, it would be an entirely consistent act for him to order them to be bumped off for security purposes, or *pour encourager les autres*, just like Jerrold, Greene and the Osgood person. Not a good career, to be a hit-man in that organization, whether you are successful or not! In all likelihood, Stoddart himself is in danger, unless he is worth more to Mr Big alive than dead! Whoever he is, this arch-villain, he seems to exercise control by fear rather than by respect. And now we have the prospect of dealing not only with rank-and-file assassins, but their senior-level counterparts, to say nothing of the supreme commander or commanders!"

After further discussion, the two agreed that they should telephone Jimmy Manley first, since they had missed returning his call the day before, and then get on to David Wilkinson.

"And, though this is less urgent," said Daphne, "it would be good to let Norman Felton know what Tessa McPherson told us about lactic acid or whatever was used on the yarn. We still have to follow up this lead, too! What with sabotage as well as murder this is getting to be a major case for Crabbe and Crabbe – remember them, Simon?"

"And there is also the question of the Packard car!" said Simon, "I would like to sort that out, if only for my own satisfaction. I don't know about you, Daphne, but I find myself thinking that there is an American connection here somewhere, what with the shooting and so on." "Or else a French one!" said Daphne.

Chapter 37

When Detective-Sergeant Manley was telephoned, he said that the reason that he had asked them to call him back the day before was that Superintendent Wilkinson had just let him know about the discovery of the bodies in the barn. Simon told him they had read the story in the newspaper that morning, and Jimmy confirmed that it was substantially true. "We are waiting for the autopsy results," he said, "Andover hospital ought to think about reserving a special laboratory just for our customers!"

"And we have a report for you!" Simon added, and related the incident at the dinner party.

"I'll contact the Huddersfield police," Jimmy said, "and get a watch put on this Stoddart – but strictly under cover – we might use him to lead us to the principals in this conspiracy, and we wouldn't want to alert them at all. By the way, we eventually traced the Packard motorcar through the number that your friend Holdsworthy was smart enough to record, and found that it is registered – wait for it – to the same Mr. Feather, at the Fillmore Gardens, Greenwich address. So that's somewhat of a dead end, seeing we did a thorough but fruitless search for him last time. Nevertheless, of course, we shall keep the file open."

"I haven't mentioned this before," said Simon, "but we noticed a Packard being stored at Prestige Automobiles in Huddersfield. I didn't get a look at the number, and of course, even though Packards may not be common in this country, there is no real reason why it has to be the same car that Jerrold and Greene were abducted in."

"Good, Simon, I'll get that followed up, too. Every little scrap of information might turn out to be valuable in the end."

"You're right, Jimmy – you should be a detective! Daphne and I – I'm getting quite used to her new name now – are going to see whether we can find out more about the lactic acid or whatever it was that was used on the yarns from Fenster and Churchman, of Leeds. We know now that Stoddart is a manager there, so it should be possible to find out whether he had anything to do with a purchase of lactic acid – or one of the others that Tessa McPherson mentioned, from Hughes and Patterson – or any other supplier, really – but H and P are most likely, since they are close by in Leeds."

"Good, Simon, nice to talk to you – say 'hello' to your lovely partner for me – I'm off to continue ticking off my long list of tasks – some of them ordinary humdrum policing! I'll let you know if anything of interest emerges from the post-mortem."

Said Daphne, "We mustn't forget to bring Norman Felton up to speed. Shall I phone him now, or is there anything else more pressing? Very well, I'll give him a call."

He was called to the telephone at Gormsby's and when Daphne had finished telling him what they had found out from Tessa McPherson, he said, "You know, we get some of our supplies from Hughes and Patterson – not lactic acid, since we have no use for it here – but, for example, cleaning agents, or the specialized lubricants we use on our looms on those moving parts that come into contact with the yarns and finished goods. If you handle cottons from the East, say, you can often smell the distinctive odour of paraffin – while you never can with good quality products, such as those from Gormsby's. What I am thinking is that our purchasing people are probably on working terms with their connections at Hughes and Patterson, and nobody would believe it odd if they asked them some questions."

"That suggests a promising approach!" said Daphne, "You could brief one of your buyers to, shall we say, point out an apparent discrepancy, saying you have been sent a consignment of lactic acid, when you never use the stuff, and see where that leads."

"Or else," said Simon, taking the telephone from her, "they could just barge straight in and ask if they had sold any of these acids recently to Fenster and Churchman's. That sort of a query is hardly likely to get back to Stoddart, is it? You are better able than us to work something out, since you're in the business, so we'll leave the details to you. Please get back to our office number in London if you come up with any promising results – we're not sure how much longer we'll be staying in the North, and there'll always be someone in the office."

Simon made a quick call to Superintendent Wilkinson – he was out of the station, so they left a message to the effect that everybody seemed up-to-date and that all they were waiting for were the post-mortem reports if they came up with anything significant.

Then he said to Daphne, "You know, while we're in Huddersfield we should try and find out about the other mills in the Winstanley group. Norman said he would speak to the managers he knows, but I'd like to have a poke round myself. I wonder if that Dr Kenneth Bullock at the University, who referred us to Tessa McPherson, would be able to help. I have his number in my book, so I'll give him a call."

Simon rang the number and was answered by someone with a strong local accent, "Dr Bullock int in at t'moment, but happen 'e'll be yer soonish – 'e's got they students coomin' in at half ten. Can I get 'im to call you then, like?"

Simon thanked the man, gave him his number and said he would wait for the call, asking him to tell Dr Bullock that it was Simon Tonkins, who he spoke to yesterday.

He rang back almost immediately, saying, "How did you get on with Tessa? I imagine she was right on the ball! Can I do anything further for you? I'll have to hurry you a bit, I'm due to introduce the next part of my vac course in a few minutes."

"Well, I'll get straight to the point, then. We, Daphne and I, would like to find a way of visiting some mills soon – particularly the two weaving mills here in the Winstanley group, and also, perhaps, Fenster and Churchman in Leeds – that is a spinning mill, I understand?"

Bullock laughed, "If you would like to join my class, we're scheduled to visit Frampton and Nunn, one of the Winstanley mills, this very afternoon, and we're going by bus to Leeds tomorrow to see spinning mills, F and C included – you must be psychic! What I've got here is a group just about to start their second year with my subject, 'Textile Machinery and Production Techniques'. Many of our students come from families who have been in the industry for ages, but we run this vacation course as a 'catch-up' for those without that inside knowledge. If you'd like to come my office, in the Queensgate technology building at 1.30, I'll lend you dust-coats and caps. Has Daphne got long hair? If so she'll need a snood! Anyone will tell you how to get to Queensgate."

Simon thanked him effusively, rang off and filled Daphne in.

"How about that for luck?" "We could do with it!" said she.

Chapter 38

They had no difficulty finding the Queensgate building; they dropped into Prestige Automobiles to let their young contact know – his name turned out to be Lester Formby – that they would not be able to pick up the Alvis yet; he told them where the building was and suggested they leave the Riley with him and walk, since the parking at the University was sometimes problematic, and it wasn't far.

They were at Kenneth Bullock's office in good time, and he greeted them cordially. He was not as he sounded on the telephone, Daphne said quietly to Simon – he was shortish and bald – but pleasant withal. He found long brown dustcoats for them – his was grey – and matching caps. He looked quizzically at Daphne's hair and finally said, "Well you'd better have a snood, to be safe, even though there's not much chance of those tight curls getting caught in the works. And put a pair of these safety glasses in your pockets – I'll tell you when they are needed."

He led them down the corridor to a small lecture room, where there were a dozen or fifteen students waiting – about a third of them girls. He made little fuss of introducing them, simply saying, "Here are a couple of visitors – if they ask any of you anything, just make up answers, like you usually do!" There was a flurry of laughter – obviously they did not hold him in any great awe.

They all settled down, mostly taking out their notebooks. Simon, of course, had his, and Daphne had just brought a pad of letter paper and two pencils. She said quietly to him, "I'm glad about the dustcoats and glasses and so on – if we happen to bump into Stoddart at any stage, he'll have a job recognizing us!"

Dr Bullock took off from a point that he had obviously reached at the end of the previous session, showing lantern slides of various pieces of machinery and commenting on them. Daphne and Simon recognized one variety of power loom, but there were others which differed from the ones at Gormsby's, both in size and layout. Bullock said he wouldn't say too much about spinning equipment until the next day, when they would visit the mills at Leeds.

It was quite interesting, though largely over Daphne and Simon's heads, and it was soon time for a little test. "Visitors are excused!" said Dr Bullock, but Daphne said that she would like to have a go anyway, so was given the same sheet as the others.

When the answers were given after half an hour, she had managed to answer at least a quarter of the questions correctly, or nearly so! "Not bad!" said Simon, who had not tried it at all!

"Good!" said Dr Bullock, "go and get something in the canteen and meet back here for the bus at 1 sharp. Latecomers will be left behind!"

Everyone managed to make the deadline, and Dr Bullock explained, "I could have walked you all over to the mill in a group, but experience tells me that we always lose a few stragglers when we do that! All aboard!"

Ten minutes later, they drove into the yard at Frampton and Nunn, and were met by a delegation of three young women, also in dustcoats, but white this time. "We'll divide into four groups," said Bullock, "otherwise some people at the back won't be able to hear the guide. I'll take one group, including our two visitors, and Miss Taylor, Miss Morris and Miss Evans will take the other three. Try and make the groups roughly equal, and off we go!"

Daphne and Simon were struck by several things that made this mill different from Gormsby's – the only other weaving mill they knew at all – the buildings were ramshackle and dusty and gave the impression they had grown over the years by having new sheds tacked on here and there, while the looms were of various different styles and sizes, in contrast to the looms at Gormsby's, which were all the same size and model, as far as they could tell.

But the most marked feature was the shouting, the noise of the machinery and the confusion of overhead shafting and belts, with stacks of cheeses and bales of finished cloth seemingly put down all over the place. As Daphne said, having to shout directly into Simon's ear, "No wonder if there is sometimes hostility between management and the owners – confusion alone could be the source of a lot of the trouble!"

After touring for an hour or so, the students were gathered together in the works canteen, where Dr Bullock asked if there were any questions. As the students were slow to speak, Daphne put up her hand and said, "I see that the weavers here are mostly women – the only men I have seen today seem to be mechanics fixing machinery, or young lads doing fetching and carrying – is this usual? Another weaving mill I have visited had mostly men weavers, but that was in the South." This prompted a male student to ask, "I saw looms that were out of service and being worked on – this would affect the efficiency of the mill, wouldn't it?"

Dr Bullock replied, "As to the women weavers, this is the usual case – if you have seen sheds with mostly male weavers, they were probably producing heavier goods. And maintenance and repairs are done mainly during wakes weeks, when most of the workers are off on their holidays at the seaside, but the looms here are getting so old – some have been working for more than forty years – that they constantly break down and have to be fixed on the run. I'm sure that management sometimes would feel tempted to burn the whole place down and start from scratch somewhere else!"

After some more questions, Dr Bullock said, "That's all for today, I'll see you in the morning. You can go on the bus back to Queensgate if you like, or just make your own way home."

Daphne and Simon got on the bus with him – a handful of students piled in, chattering among themselves, so Simon thought he would clear up some further points.

"I was quite shocked to see how disorganized this mill seemed to be – is this typical? The only other mill I've seen is Gormsby's, in Hampshire, which is notably different – the shed is laid out in orderly rows of looms, all the looms seem to be of similar make and age, the yarn spools are lined up along the walls neatly and there is plenty of light and air."

"Well, that mill was set up from scratch only a few years since, on a site in the midst of farmland – the buildings are new and so is the equipment – so it is easy to keep things running smoothly. In the south there is not the same tradition of annual wakes weeks – I believe they have a holiday roster and send their workers on leave a few rows of looms at a time, so maintenance can be done on a much more rational basis. One of my colleagues has written a paper on all this for the next World Weaving Congress, in India this December. I'll ask him if he will send you a copy, if you like."

Chapter 39

Back at the department, Kenneth Bullock said they could leave their coats and caps with him or take them as they pleased, so they left them there, thanked him and said they would be back in the morning.

As they walked back to Prestige Automobiles, Daphne said, "Although I am pining a little for the Alvis, I think it would be prudent for us to keep the Riley, along with our aliases, until we set off back to London." Simon agreed and said, "I might try to get another glimpse of that Packard – I'd like to check the number."

So, after he had told Lester Formby of the plans to pick up the car, Simon walked round to the back of the building to have a look. The Packard was there still, and he checked the number in his notebook – it was the same that Holdsworthy had noted! He stood by the car, thinking, and a mechanic came up to him saying, "Lovely cars, these. Dost tha want to sit in her for a bit?"

Simon nodded and the man opened the driver's door and waved him in. The seat was a little close to the wheel, and seeing this, the mechanic showed Simon the lever for adjusting the position, and helped him move it back a few inches. As he did this, Simon saw the corner of a scrap of paper sticking out from under the seat. He picked it up and pocketed it, without being noticed, and then listened attentively to the mechanic's explanation of all the controls, which were different from those usual in British cars.

He thanked him and said, "Bit too expensive for me, I'm afraid – you'd need to be a rich man to afford to run one of these."

"That'd be right! Mr Pilkington wouldn't be short of a bob or two, what wi' his foundry, his department store and lord knows what else!"

Simon went round to the showroom, where Daphne was chatting with Lester, asked him where was a good place for afternoon tea, and was directed to the Lyons Corner House.

Apart from tea – China for Daphne and Ceylon for Simon – they tucked into, respectively, a double fudge sundae and anchovies on toast. "We may regret this when we find we have no appetite for dinner!" said Simon, while Daphne replied, "Not a chance!"

Sitting back from the table, satisfied, Simon remembered the paper, which turned out to have printing on one side and handwriting on the other, which read: *'You know the two lawyers by sight. They usually drink in 'The White Rose', near Weavers Mansions. Hang out there every night until they turn up. Grab them without violence if you can. Put them in the car and make sure they don't run. Parker knows where to go.'*

It bore no signature. Both exclaimed, almost together, "The instructions for the kidnappers!" and "The thugs' marching orders!", and Daphne went on, "This settles it – that Packard is definitely part of the plot – we really need to find out more about the mysterious Mr Pilkington!"

"We could bring in the West Yorkshire police at this point," said Simon, but that would mean an awful lot of explanation, verifying that we are bona fide and so on. I think we should call on Jimmy Manley once again." Daphne agreed readily, and added, "What about the back of the note?"

The other side seemed to be part of a bill, with the top part torn off, and some cryptic entries, like:

'46 THERMS BASIC TARIFF

102 THERMS CONCESSIONAL RATE

TOTAL FOR PERIOD £14/10/9'

At the bottom there was what could have been a serial number:

'ADE 524271911'

"What is this all about?" said Simon. "No idea!" replied Daphne, "Therms sounds a bit scientific to me, perhaps we could ask Tessa or Kenneth Bullock?"

"We don't even know whether this is a Huddersfield bill, or one from London." Said Simon, "This is not going to be all that easy to trace!"

It seemed to be a good time to phone Detective-Sergeant Manley before he went off duty, so as soon as they were back in their room in the hotel, Simon asked for his number to be called. The woman on the hotel switchboard said "You're running up quite a bill, you know!", but put him through quite quickly.

He related all the significant events of the day – Jimmy was, of course, principally interested in the alleged ownership of the Packard, the note to the villains and the supposed bill. "We intend to find out what therms means," said Simon, "we thought that Dr McPherson might be able to tell us."

Jimmy laughed at that, "It's obvious that neither of you have ever been concerned very much with domestic arrangements! What you've got there is a gas bill – therms are simply a measure of the volume of gas that you use. Once we've found out which gas company we're dealing with, the serial number will probably tell us heaps! Just leave that to us, I'm sure DC Thompson will enjoy tracking it down! And while he's doing that, I'll see what I can find out from the West Yorkshire Police about the sinister – or at least mysterious – Mr Pilkington."

They thanked him and rang off.

"Now I want to try out an idea on Norman," said Daphne, "do you have his home number in your little book? Good – let's see if he's knocked off work yet."

Melinda answered, and Daphne remembered to use the name Melpomene to her, even though it was beginning to sound strange! Norman wasn't home yet, so she asked Melinda if he would kindly call her at the hotel as soon as convenient after nine o'clock, saying, "We'll probably be at dinner before that. It's not urgent, I just want to bounce some ideas off him!"

But just as they had freshened up and changed and were about to go to the dining room, he did ring.

"Good evening, Norman!" she said, "We have lots to tell you, but I will save it up for now. I just want to get your reactions to a hypothetical situation. It's this – suppose there is a wealthy investor whose money is tied up in several weaving and spinning mills that are past their prime, are no longer profitable, and starting to lose him money. He has his eye on a modern weaving mill that is efficient and profitable but whose shares would fetch a high price on the market. Being a dishonest and unscrupulous man, he decides he will ruin its profitability and drive down its share values. He can afford to spend several years doing this, and when the reputation of that mill has been destroyed and it value reduced he will acquire the shares of the mill and thus control over its operation, and will be the proud owner of a flourishing concern – once he has stopped sabotaging it! What do you think, Norman?"

117

Chapter 40

Norman Felton paused for a few moments, then replied, but in a somewhat doubtful tone, "I shall have to think about this at some length, Melpomene, but I have two initial reactions. First, you may well have something here, and second, even if we or our police contacts manage to identify the person or persons involved, what can be done about it? If that someone is as resourceful and unscrupulous as you imply then we have little chance of either revealing what is going on, or of subsequently fighting it through the courts – we suspect that he has already resorted to murder – several times! But leave these thoughts with me – I assume that you are not intending to take direct action yet?"

"You are right, Norman," replied Daphne, "I just wanted to give you the opportunity to start thinking about this as a possibility – it's all guesswork so far! We'll catch up with you tomorrow evening, if that's all right, there are a few developments we want you to know about. But we're off to dinner, now!"

Over dinner, Simon and Daphne summed up the new information that they had, and discussed what they might do on their tour of Fenster and Churchman the next day. As Simon said, they would simply have to play it by ear, and seize any chance that came up to find out more. "Of course," said Daphne, "we might or might not bump into Stoddart – we didn't come across any management people at that mill today – but if we do run across him, I think that our dustcoats, caps – and possibly safety glasses, too – ought to be sufficient disguise. And anyway he was somewhat distracted last time we met, was he not – I wonder what state he'll be in tomorrow?"

"If he hasn't been bumped off in the meantime!" added Simon, with a wry grin.

Feeling rather aroused mentally, Daphne decided that another dose of Ethel M Dell was indicated before bedtime, but Simon needed no such soporific, simply had a bath and went straight to bed.

After breakfast, Daphne asked, "Shall we phone Jimmy Manley before we go this morning?" Simon thought for a moment and said, "No, let's leave it until after we've been to Leeds and back, then if we find out anything we'll be able to tell him. Besides, it will give DC Thompson longer to track down the gas bill."

After a short talk to the students by Kenneth Bullock, and a snack and tea in the college refectory, they and the students got on the bus at about 11 am and set out on the Leeds road. They recognized one or two landmarks they had seen previously when they were driving to Huddersfield, including an elegant stone mansion set well back from the road in landscaped grounds. Daphne, who was sitting next to Kenneth, pointed it out, saying, "That's an impressive place, is it the seat of a noble family?"

His reply, accompanied by a dismissive grunt, was, "The current owner would certainly aspire to the nobility, but as yet he is merely one of our prominent local captains of commerce and industry, Francis Josiah Pilkington. He started out working in his father's grocer's shop, and worked his way upwards and outwards – not always in the most admirable ways. He now owns that place, Flockton Hall, which indeed used to be the seat of Lord Flockton of Doncaster, as well as prosperous department stores in Huddersfield, Bradford and Leeds and more than one woollen mill. He is not a popular figure in West Yorkshire!"

"Why is that?" asked Daphne. "The whole region", explained Kenneth, "is littered, figuratively speaking, with his victims – honest folk who have lost their businesses and not-so-honest ones who did not play the game as ruthlessly as they needed to in order to compete with him and his cronies!"

Daphne was aware that Simon, seated directly behind them, was scribbling in his little book.

The trip to Fenster and Churchman's works on the outskirts of Leeds took little more than half an hour, and they all disembarked in the yard of the mill. Dr Bullock announced that they would tour in one large group this time, explaining, "A spinning mill is not as noisy as a weaving shed, and anyway there's lot more technical explanation required, and I like to do that myself. There are many stages that the wool passes through from fleece to yarn, and the mill is laid out so we can follow the process from the sheep's back to yours in a logical order. Who can list these processes?"

Two students, a boy and a girl, put their hands up, and Bullock said, "We'll take you first, Brenda Collins, and Alastair can take

119

over if you leave anything out. OK, Brenda, what stage comes first?"

"The fleeces are skirted first, to take off the dags, then they are scoured to get them clean – if there is any vegetable matter, it is removed with acid – this has a special name which I have forgotten – Alastair, what is it? Ah yes, carbonising. Then there is oiling, carding and combing into roving and then it is ready for final spinning into yarn. Is that right, Dr Bullock?"

"Not bad, Brenda – when it comes to the exam, you'll have to tidy it up a bit, though, and spend more time describing the stages in detail. Well done for now! We'll have a cup of tea, and if I remember right, the canteen here has Eccles cakes! And I'll call you together then for the tour."

Daphne and Simon found that this mill was much less disorganized and untidy than yesterday's weaving mill, and they were able, with the benefit of Brenda's description, to follow the progress of the wool through the system. As they approached the scouring shop, Kenneth Bullock told them all to put their safety glasses on, saying, "If you have ever had caustic soda or even soap splashed in your eyes, you'd know why!"

When they had finally reached the shed where the spinning machines were working, Simon drew Daphne's attention to a storage space, surrounded by a wire partition, within which could be seen rows of what they recognized must be carboys.

She touched Dr Bullock's sleeve and said, "What would be in those, Kenneth?" "I'm not absolutely sure, you'd have to peer at the labels – they are probably part of what is used for scouring, or maybe for bleaching – I could ask if you are specially interested." "Oh, no, just wondering!"

Then he told the group, "The works manager here likes to address students who have toured his mill – partly just as a courtesy, but partly because he is trying to attract later year students to participate in their vacation training. I think they have some recruitment difficulties here."

They were all taken into a lecture room where there were three or four senior staff, as well as the works manager, who made his speech. And standing at the back of that group, looking tired and grey, was Michael Stoddart!

"He's here, but what good that information is to us, I don't know," whispered Daphne.

Chapter 41

The works manager gave out one piece of information that interested Daphne and Simon, "If you saw one or two people in white coats wandering around during your tour, you may have wondered what they were doing. They are government inspectors on a periodic visit, checking for child labour abuse, dangerous machinery, fire precautions and so on. I am glad to say that our mill has a very good all-round record."

Daphne whispered to Simon, "I'm going to slip out while this is going on and have a bit of a snoop round – I'll meet you back at the bus if I don't get back here before he stops waffling!"

She left the room quietly and tried to retrace her steps back to the spinning room. She found the enclosure with the carboys and peered through the wire at the labels. Most of them were labelled '10% NaOH' or similar, which she recognized from school chemistry lessons as caustic soda, probably used in scouring, she thought. But then she was pleased to see one labelled, 'Lactic acid: descaling and soap-scum removal – dilute before use.' There was more detail on the label, but as she stood up to take out her notepaper, a man approached, saying, "Can I help you, miss? Are you with the college tour group?"

"Yes I am!" she said, "Can you tell me the way to the ladies' lavatory, please?"

He smiled and directed her back the way she had come. She slipped back into the lecture room – without visiting the toilet – and saw that people were getting ready to leave. "Anything interesting?" she asked Simon, "Tell you later!" he replied, and they walked back to the bus with all the others.

They took one of the back seats in the bus, and Simon said, "Just after you left, a woman, maybe a typist, came in and spoke to Stoddart. He looked annoyed, but went out with her – that's it! No farther forward, I'm afraid." She told him about the lactic acid, and he nodded.

As they neared the Pilkington mansion, a big black car – not a Packard – drew out of the gates and took off fast in the direction they were heading. Daphne said quietly, "I don't suppose we can tell the bus-driver 'Follow that car and don't let it out of your sight!' like they do in the pictures, what a pity!"

"I couldn't get the number," said Simon, "and I'm not even sure of the make!

When they left the bus at the University, they thanked Kenneth Bullock and promised to let him know any further developments, then Daphne asked, "Is there one of Pilkington's renowned Department stores here in Huddersfield – I would like to have a look at it if so?"

"Why yes, walk up that street there past the Post Office and turn left, and you can't miss it, good luck!"

The shop front was obviously an attempt to reproduce one of the large West End establishments, even to the décor inside. Daphne perused the directory on the wall by the lift and told Simon she might try the haute couture salon advertised as occupying the top floor. "Let me see what the Huddersfield idea of high fashion might be!" Simon said, "Forgive me if I don't join you, I intend to head for the brasserie on the third floor, where I shall partake of a coffee and maybe a pastry. Join me there when you have finished drooling over outfits you cannot afford. Maybe we can dine here if the menu looks passable."

Daphne pressed the button for the lift, and the door was soon opened by an elderly man in a buttoned uniform. "Top floor, Madam, is it? And you sir, the same?" Simon told him "No, the brasserie, please." The lift jolted into motion, and the attendant said, sotto voce, mainly to himself, "When are you going to fix this, then, Mr P – once you've enjoyed your trip to gay Paree?", then in a louder voice, "Third floor: Resterong, Gents' Clothes Shoes and Hats, and Gardenin' Tools!" Simon got out.

As the attendant pressed the button for the fourth floor, Daphne noticed that there was a further button above, with a Yale-type keyhole by its side. Never shy, she asked the old man, "What's on the fifth floor then?", to which he growled. "That's his office and flat – old man Pilkington! But if I ever dared to stop there, there'd be 'ell to pay!"

She got out on the fourth floor – "Hort Cooter, Ladies Hairdressing, Beauty Salong" – and wandered into the room just as a model girl was sweeping through an audience of mainly elderly ladies sitting on gilt chairs. She was dressed in an outfit that Daphne guessed was meant to be worn in the members' enclosure at Pontefract races, and was followed by another young woman in a gown suitable for a debutante being presented to the Queen. Daphne decided that the modes on offer here were not for her, and left. In the lift foyer, she noticed a door marked "Fire Stairs: Keep Closed" and on an impulse went over and pushed it open. It gave onto the promised fire stairs, and there was a flight leading upward. "I wonder ... " she thought, and started to climb. There was a double turn and then another landing with a door corresponding to the one below.

She gingerly pushed it open, peering through the gap, but saw only a corridor. Unlike the passages in the store, however, it was softly carpeted, and the walls were papered with a rich dark red design, giving it the air of an expensive hotel. She stepped through and then her ears were assailed by the loud ringing of an alarm bell, startling her so that she let go of the door, which slammed behind her.

The next thing she knew was being gripped painfully by the arm and hustled along by a tall powerful man, while a second brandished a pistol in her face. She was pushed down onto a chair next to a small table, and, while his companion went out again, the armed man kept his gun pointed at her, saying, "I won't give you no guesses what'll 'appen to you if you gives any trouble. Sit quiet and only speak when you're spoken to!"

After a wait that seemed endless, the first bruiser entered, bringing two men with him. One was short, dressed expensively but flashily, like, Daphne thought, a tycoon in a Hollywood thriller, even with the stub of a black cigar in his mouth, and the other, Daphne saw, was Michael Stoddart! She tried to look away, but she could tell it was too late!

He grinned wearily and said, "Well, well, if it isn't Daphne Tonkins – also known as Melpomene Crabbe, partner in the firm of Crabbe and Crabbe, Private Investigators! May I introduce Mr Francis Josiah Pilkington!"

Pilkington took the seat facing Melpomene, grinned a twisted grin and said in a accent that was on its way from village Yorkshire to refined English, but not quite there yet, "So, we meet at last – I do believe you and your hubby, not to mention half the British Police Force, have been looking for me. Well, I have to tell you, finding me is one thing, pinning anything on me is quite another!"

"Now, Stoddart, you know you owe me, what do you suggest we do to find out what this young lady knows?"

Chapter 42

"Why not just ask her?" suggested Stoddart, "If she jibs at anything, this'll be telling, too! And she's realistic enough to know she can't easily lie, because she doesn't know what we know already!"

Meanwhile, two floors down in the brasserie, Simon looked at his watch rather anxiously – it had been nearly an hour since they parted. So paying for the coffee, which had unexpectedly been rather good, and the apple pie, which had been rather like cardboard, he headed for the lift and pressed the 'up' button.

The lift attendant, recognising him, said, "Making sure your lady don't spend all your money, eh?" and then, recalling the conversation about the extra button, said, "I hope she took my advice and didn't try the fifth floor – old Pilkington gets very touchy about people going up there – I'm only allowed to let off people what have the right key!"

Simon ventured into 'haute couture' but, seeing that she wasn't there, tried the hairdressing salon and the beauty parlour, of course drawing blanks there too. He went back to the lift and called it again. He said to the attendant, "Are you sure my wife didn't go down again – have you been on duty all the time?" and was assured that she certainly didn't use the lift again. "Is this the only lift?" has asked, "Oh yes, sir, but there's fire stairs o' course – there's the door over there!"

Simon decided that he wouldn't embark on what might become a wild-goose chase, so asked for the ground floor. There was a floor-walker near the lift, not doing very much, so Simon asked, "Have you seen a pretty young lady, about so tall, with fair curls, wearing a sleeveless dress in green chiffon, in a flower print?" but the man rather haughtily said that he had not, but might not remember anyway, "Most of our customers are pretty and well-dressed, sir!"

Getting more and more anxious, Simon decided to go to the authorities, so asked for directions to the nearest police station, which was less than five minutes' walk away. He told the desk sergeant he would like to report a missing person, and was directed to a small office, where a policewoman soon appeared, carrying a sheaf of forms. He gave his real name and address, and as he was giving Melpomene's particulars, the WPC said,

"That unusual name rings a bell! Excuse me for a moment." She left and returned shortly after with a man in plain clothes. "I'm Detective-Inspector Walter Simmonds," he said, "and there is already an alert out which mentions both your and your wife's names as interested parties, with Detective-Sergeant Manley of the Met and Superintendent Wilkinson of Hampshire Constabulary as professional contacts. Manley is listed as coordinator. Now WPC Farsley has just told me that your immediate concern is that your wife, Melpomene Crabbe, has recently gone missing. In the ordinary course of business, we do not follow up missing person reports immediately – for obvious reasons – they often turn up by themselves – but in this case, since it is an active enquiry, we must lose no time. So please give me the particulars, as fully as possible."

When Alex had finished, Simmonds asked, "Have you any theories, no matter how wild, as to what might have happened? You have been immersed in this business for much longer than us, and you are a private investigator, too – some police have problems with private detectives, but I do not!"

"My first thought is that Pilkington has something to do with it!" said Alex, "We have both begun to think that he is behind a lot of the skulduggery, including murders, that are surrounding this case. We have various bits of evidence to support this idea, but nothing so far that would stand up in a court of law. Have you been in contact with DS Manley at Mile End Road lately? He was following up a clue written on the back of a gas bill, which appeared to be instructions for the abduction of the two murdered lawyers who were fished out of the docks!"

"Let's check with Jimmy Manley straight away!" said Simmonds, and picked up the phone, "Hello, Julie, see if you can get DS Manley at Mile End Road for me. It is quite urgent, so he can be interrupted if necessary!"

"While we're waiting," said Simmonds, "I'll bring you up to date on the charming Mr Pilkington. As you may have gathered, he is not the most popular man in the West Riding, and we have been trying to pin a number of offences on him for a year or two – burglaries, frauds, improper company transactions, unwarranted dismissals and so on, and even importation of prescribed goods and illegal immigrants – quite a list. But he is as cunning as a fox and twice as cruel. He has a number of residences listed, which have been visited by the police on a number of occasions, and even searched sometimes, but nothing incriminating has ever been found, nor have any criminal associates ever been seen with him."

The phone rang, and Simmonds picked it up, "Jimmy, old man, Wally Simmonds here – are you keeping the villains at bay down your way? I have Alex Crabbe with me, worried sick because Melpomene has vanished. Have you got anywhere with your enquiries around the notorious gas bill? You have? Your DC Thompson has done well! Tell me all about it, while I take notes."

He listened, nodding and sometimes asking for more details, then said, "Wonderful, Jimmy – please get onto it straight away! If he's headed for home, it'll take him at least two hours, even in one of his fast cars, and Melpomene was last seen – what is it, an hour ago – so your blokes have got maybe an hour to get into position. Over to you!"

He hung up and turned back to Alex, who had been on the edge of his seat.

"That gas bill has paid dividends!" he said, "DC Thompson tried nearly a dozen gas companies between Huddersfield and London, and the serial number matched the West Essex Gas Company, that supplies an area from London to the north and east. The bill was issued by an office in Brentwood, and further enquiries came up with the name and address of the customer. Tearing the top off the bill was not enough, because the file entry for that serial number had their full name and address!"

"Here it is: Mr and Mrs James Willoughby, Kynaston Court, Chelsfield Lane, Brentwood. This is a large modern house on about a quarter of an acre on the outskirts of the town, with a number of outbuildings, including a three-car garage. As you can gather, Jimmy's men have already staked it out, and now they will set up a comprehensive surveillance operation."

"Should I drive down there?" asked Alex. "I wouldn't advise it," said Simmonds, "we are only surmising so far that Melpomene has been taken south. You'd be better off staying at your hotel, which is where she will try to get in touch with you if she gets a chance. I gather from DS Manley that she is a very resourceful lady, with a few tricks up her sleeve!"

So Alex walked to Prestige Automobiles, checked that the Packard was still there, picked up the Alvis, which Lester said was now "in top-notch condition" and drove to the hotel.

Chapter 43

At Huddersfield Central Police Station, DI Simmonds got a message from one of his men stationed outside the back of the department store, who had been keeping an eye on Pilkington's car, parked there since it had arrived earlier. He said that Pilkington, and two of his heavies apparently holding up a woman who was walking unsteadily, had just come out of the back entrance and got into the car. As previously instructed, the officer had kept out of sight but noticed that at the main street they had turned towards the Leeds road.

Simmonds made sure that DS Manley would get this information as soon as possible, so that the surveillance team at the Brentwood house would be ready. He then phoned Alex at the hotel and said that it looked likely that Melpomene was on her way south. He forbore to mention that she had been seen walking unsteadily.

"If you drive to Brentwood," he said, "Jimmy Manley has set up an incident room at the local nick, in the town centre. You had better check in there when you arrive – don't on any account go to the Pilkington house before finding out the situation, please."

"Of course not!" replied Alex, "I've got a lot of confidence in Detective-Sergeant Manley!"

In the event, it was nearly half past six before he got there, glad that he had not been clocked by the police driving at high speed anywhere along the route. He was welcomed by Jimmy, who told him that the car of interest had arrived at Kynaston Court not long before.

"My blokes saw the car turn into the gates," he said, "and drive straight into the garage closest to the house, the doors shutting behind it. They could not see who then went into the house, because of a high privet hedge, but they heard some shouted conversations and then the slamming of a door."

"So what will you do next?" asked Alex, rather anxiously, "Who knows what they might be doing to Melpomene now!"

"One of my men, DC Jock MacFee – a Scotsman with deer-stalking experience, would you believe – is going to see what is visible through the windows. There is plenty of greenery around the house, so he ought to be able to do this without being spotted – as long as there are no burglar alarms, of course! Let's go to the house now – my team are all waiting in a fishmonger's van just round the corner, where they can see the gates, but not the house itself."

Manley's driver parked just behind the van, and Jimmy and Alex knocked on the rear door and were admitted, to be met by a blast of hot air, scented with cigarette smoke and elderly fish.

"You'll all need decontaminating before your families will let you back in your homes!" said Jimmy, "What developments so far? Is Jock back yet?"

But before anyone could answer, there was the unmistakeable sound of a burglar alarm coming from the house, closely followed by two pistol shots!

Jimmy jumped down from the van, blowing his whistle and then shouting, "Everybody in, as quickly as possible! Axes ready and break the doors down if you have to!"

He and two of his men took the front door, with Alex following. They could hear shouting from the back of the house, too, and the sound of breaking windows.

Alex and his companions barged the front doors aside with their shoulders and found themselves in a hallway, with rooms opening off it on both sides. At the far end of the hall, more policemen appeared, some with their truncheons at the ready. Alex drew his Luger, cocked it and took off the safety.

And then, out of a door on the left came Melpomene, holding a pistol and grinning like a Cheshire cat!

Everybody was frozen to the spot, and then she said, "Someone had better call an ambulance, there are two men bleeding freely in there! But Mr Pilkington is not one of them, I don't know where he can have got to!"

Jimmy and another policeman opened the door cautiously and then relaxed. As Melpomene had said, there were two rough-looking men, one lying on the floor groaning, and the other slumped on a chair, trying to hold his trousers together to staunch the flow of blood from his thigh. Jimmy went back to the hallway, calling, "Who has a recent St. John's certificate – there are two patients here who need tourniquets and bandages or we'll lose them! The rest of you, start a thorough search of the house, upstairs and down, and I mean thorough – don't miss a single cupboard or wardrobe, and find out if there's an attic or a cellar. We're looking for someone who might act in desperation, so watch yourselves!"

Then Melpomene said quietly, "Can someone make me a cup of sweet tea, please, I think I'm about to have a nervous reaction to all this!"

Alex took her to another room, which turned out to be a sitting-room, and settled her on a couch with her feet up. Then a resourceful constable appeared from the back of the house with a huge steaming mug and a biscuit-barrel. "Nobody in the kitchen or scullery, Sergeant!" he announced, "And all the outside doors are covered!"

Melpomene sipped her tea, and then Alex said, "Try and have a nap, my darling, we can all wait till later to hear all about it!" He sat by her side, patting her gently while she dropped off, and then put his head out into the hallway to see what was happening.

Jimmy was standing on a bottom stair, carrying on a conversation with someone out of sight above. "We've got someone in an upstairs lavatory – he's holding the door to keep us out and he's swearing like a scandinavian lorry-driver!"

"Hang on, I'll come up," said Jimmy, but then they heard the sound of breaking glass. "He's trying to get out of the window," said the man who'd been trying to open the door with his mate. "So bust the door down, quick!" said Jimmy.

They did so, meeting no resistance this time, and then the first one in burst out laughing, "He's stuck in the window – he needs to go on a diet before he tries that again! Come on, matey, let's have you!" The two pulled and heaved at his legs, and then dragged him into the hall, blubbering like a child, red-faced and exhausted.

Jimmy pulled his arms behind his back, and handcuffed him, saying, "Francis Josiah Pilkington, I arrest you in the name of the King. A list of charges will be read to you when you are arraigned."

Alex thought that this was a suitable reason to wake Melpomene, telling her, "We've got the chief villain, darling – you can tell us all what happened later! Go back to sleep now, if you can!"

Chapter 44

The two injured men were taken by ambulance to the local hospital, where they were treated further for their wounds and had their bullets extracted, carefully labelled and boxed and given into the hands of the police. The emergency-room doctor said to the two constables assigned to guard them, "Next time you or your colleagues shoot somebody, try to get qualified help before you attempt to treat them at the scene. A tourniquet might be helpful in the case of snake-bite, but it is not the best way of staunching bleeding. Never mind, though, these men will recover and are not likely to sue!"

They were soon handcuffed to their beds in a small ward, under the eye of a policeman, looking very subdued, but no longer in severe pain.

As for Pilkington, he was taken to the lock-up at the local police station to be held until he, as well as his injured associates, could be brought before a magistrate and formally charged. He had stopped crying but looked very sorry for himself.

The house, Kynaston Court, was secured as much as possible, and several police were stationed there until all possible evidence could be discovered and gathered. A strong-room had been found in the cellar and this had been sealed until it could be opened by experts.

While all this activity was going on, Jimmy Manley suggested that the best place for Melpomene would be her own flat, and that, if she and Alex would have him, he could come there too, with a police shorthand writer in attendance, so that when she felt ready she could relate her story in familiar surroundings.

Melpomene said that she was very comfortable with that, and added, "Why don't we telephone ahead and ask Caroline and Mrs M to rustle up a decent meal for us and our two guests? I suppose we can be there in less than an hour, can't we? For some reason I am incredibly hungry, and I don't feel like eating out!"

"You can grab a rock-cake from the canteen if you like!" said Jimmy, "and eat it in my squad car, as long as you don't drop crumbs! I don't suppose you're ready for your Alvis yet."

"I'll see you all at the flat, then!" said Alex, and they all set off. Jimmy's shorthand writer, a young policewoman, asked if she might travel with Alex, as she had "never ridden in a flash car like that!" and he agreed. "If I'm stopped for speeding now, I'll be able to claim I'm on official police business, won't I?"

When they arrived at the flat, Caroline and Mrs M apologized for the meal, saying that the notice they had been given was rather short, so "All we could manage was chicken cacciatori and spaghetti, with tinned apricots and ice-cream to follow." However, both Jimmy and Melpomene said that they had done very well, considering, and would enjoy it with great pleasure, Alex agreed, saying he hadn't had that dish for long time and really liked it.

After dinner, they took their glasses of wine or cups of tea to the sitting room. WPC Jennifer Sweet, the shorthand writer, settled herself on an upright chair with her pad and pencil, and the others found somewhere comfortable.

Melpomene began, "For a few moments, after I had set off the alarm outside Pilkington's suite in the store, I scolded myself bitterly for poking my nose in where it was not wanted, but I soon saw this was pointless. Then, as soon as I was grabbed by the two henchmen, I decided to play soppy and feminine, which I reckoned was what they would expect of a young, middle-class, blonde-headed woman, and tried to look as though I might faint any moment."

"Hah!" murmured Alex, and Jimmy smiled, too.

"Pilkington then came in, to my great surprise bringing with him Michael Stoddart, who proceeded to blow my cover, greeting me by my proper name as well as Daphne. But I still meant to stick to my guns – even if Stoddart was not fooled, his opinion would hardly be taken any notice of by the others. Pilkington, of course, despises everybody, not just silly women! Our second year psychology classes had covered various personality defects, and I diagnosed him as a clear-cut example of narcissism."

Alex explained to the others at this point that, "Mel tends to get all theoretical under stress – this is called the 'ignore reality' syndrome!" Melpomene glared at him and he made a funny face and shut up.

"If I may continue?" Mel went on, "Pilkington then told Stoddart is was up to him to make me talk. I had the impression he has some sort of hold over him – Stoddart was still looking very stressed. Anyway, Stoddart then told the two heavies to hold me down and produced a small bottle and some rags – I don't mind telling you, I thought of nicotine and my heart sank, but then I got a whiff of it – it was chloroform! He poured some into a rag and held it over my face"

The audience was certainly paying attention at this point, and WPC Sweet was scribbling furiously.

Melpomene continued, "It's strange how one's mind works under stress – I thought 'just like Theda Bara in the Secret of Dr Fu Manchu' – so I behaved as she did in the picture, I rolled my eyes up so the whites would show – but the difference was that I held my breath and only inhaled a trace of the chloroform. Then I went all limp and pretended I had passed out! That rotten Stoddart pinched my arm painfully to test me, but I managed not to react. After this is all over, I am going the rounds of the West End theatrical agencies – not including 'Global Productions' – to secure a part in the next big melodrama that is coming up."

"So tell us what happened next!" pleaded Alex, "or I shall pass out in suspense!"

"The rest was very boring!" retorted Melpomene, "I stayed as limp as I could and was bundled into the car and driven for hours. The only interesting thing was that one of the thugs was sitting next to me in the back seat, and I kept sagging onto him – and that's how I found he was carrying his pistol in a shoulder holster, just like Alex – I had spotted that it was a Luger, too!"

"After a long trip, we arrived at the house and I was half-carried into a room. By this time, my guards were getting tired and careless, and they just propped me up on a settee – the one with the Luger sitting next to me half asleep with his jacket off, and the other one pacing about. When the burglar alarm went off, my escort roused himself with a start to see what it was, and I purloined his pistol! As the other one turned and started to make a lunge at me, I took off the safety, cocked it and shot him in the thigh! I enjoyed this so much that I did the same to his partner! I'm kidding of course – he made a grab at me as well so I had to stop him too. The rest is history, as they say!"

Chapter 45

Detective-Sergeant Manley clapped, applauding this narrative, and saying, "Melpomene, my congratulations! You have obtained results that the rest of us have been striving toward for a long time – but, however, at considerable personal risk – we could easily have lost you! Please don't be so daring in the future!"

"Hear, hear!" said Alex.

"The next stage," continued Jimmy, "is to gather evidence to convict our various captives. Melpomene by herself can certainly provide, as an eye-witness and victim, convincing facts to support charges of kidnapping or deprivation of liberty, not to mention assault, all of these warranting long jail sentences, but what I and many others would really like would be to get Pilkington and several of his minions on one or more of a series of capital murder charges – I, for one, think he and some of his accomplices deserve to swing!"

"Laboratory tests will help – we have the gun and bullets that Mel just took from thug number 1 – no doubt we shall identify him by name in due course – and we will check these against the bullets used in the 'bodies in the barn' killings, with the comparison microscope that the Yard has recently acquired from America, like the one they used over there in the Sacco and Vanzetti case. That will be a start. Then there's the murder by nicotine poisoning of William Brooks – we have good circumstantial evidence that it was administered by Greene, but we must pursue those who provided him with it and ordered its use. And the other murder that needs following up is the drowning in the docks of Greene, Jerrold and the Osgood person. We think we have its instigator locked up, and the famous gas bill is already being examined for fingerprints, while Pilkington's handwriting will be checked against it by a Home Office forensic document examiner. Is there anything else that comes to mind at present?"

"If we could ask Jennifer Sweet to let us have a copy of her notes, once she has transcribed them and typed them up, that would be appreciated. But I reckon that all of this will satisfy us for the moment, thanks, Jimmy!" said Alex, "Will you brief the police in Huddersfield and Woodhampton about everything?

It's becoming very clear that there are still a lot of loose ends. Even though Pilkington has been safely locked away, I don't think we should make any assumptions about Stoddart and Hutchinson – as far as we know they are both threats lurking in the background – and we don't know anything much about Stoddart's wife, either."

"I couldn't agree with you more!" said Jimmy, "It is not clear yet whether Hutchinson is a principal in all this plotting or just another one of Pilkington's sidekicks. But it looks as though Stoddart has in some way fallen under his control – or at least he had until recently!"

Alex nodded at this and said, "This all confirms what I have been thinking – that Melpomene and I need a bit of a break to clear our heads as well as having a rest. Maybe we should go down to Woodhampton for a few days – and we can make sure that Norman Felton is brought up to date while we're there. The poor man could never have imagined what that incident that at first seemed like a simple break-in would eventually lead to!"

After breakfast the next day, Melpomene suggested they visit the office before they set off for Woodhampton. "Marjorie deserves to be properly briefed about it all," she said, "and we should find out if any other business has come our way – we can't afford to have all our eggs in one basket, whatever its size!"

At the office, it took several cups of tea and many jam tarts to tell Marjorie the whole story, "You'll get a copy of the full transcript of Mel's adventures soon," promised Alex, "which would make a good article for 'Modern Tales of Detection and Intrigue', if there is such a pulp magazine! Now, what items of interest have you been dealing with back at the ranch, Marjorie?"

"Well, of course I can't come up to Melpomene's standard of excitement," said she, "but a very interesting client came in yesterday – I said I would get back to him quickly, so I'll give you the notes on his case to take away with you – I can see you're itching to be off, now! And you'll be pleased to hear that I've banked several cheques over the last couple of days – one from the Misses Atwell and a long overdue one from that lady a few months ago whose husband had been milking her private funds – she also tells us that the divorce was made final and she actually got a settlement that made him very bitter!"

Melpomene insisted on driving to Woodhampton, "You had a good long go from Huddersfield to Brentwood and beyond, after all, so its certainly my turn now!"

They stopped half way and had a light snack to keep their appetites at bay, but drove up to the hotel before noon. This time they were expected, since they has asked Marjorie to phone ahead, so they were shown to the best suite once more.

As they were unpacking, Lady Cynthia popped her head in and then came and hugged Melpomene, saying, "I believe you have had some amazing adventures since last we met – you must tell me all about it later. But for now you had better wash your faces and get ready for lunch – we have some people you know here with us today."

And as they walked into the dining room, there indeed were Norman Felton and Melinda – looking unusually calm and happy – as well as Stephen Buckmaster, Eugenie and Fiona.

They all wanted to know what the Crabbes had been up to, so Melpomene said, "I haven't yet had time to prepare the lantern slides, but I will make a full presentation to a few invited guests in the small lounge immediately after lunch. Tickets will be handed out soon!"

Both she and Alex kept their lips buttoned on that topic during lunch, since there were other guests at the tables who were strangers or slight acquaintances with no interest in what Stephen called 'matters forensic'.

The lunch met the hotel's usual high standard, and it was with a certain reluctance that they left the table and took their glasses or cups into the lounge.

Then Stephen said, "By George, Alex and Mel, I've just realised. If you've been driving down here this morning, I don't suppose you've had a chance to see the papers yet!" He went to the newspaper rack and seized a copy of one of the London papers. He displayed and read out the front page headline, "Notorious Murder Gang foiled in Essex Shoot-Out: Young Detective's Triumph!"

Everybody wanted to see, but Mel said, "Just wait for the authentic story, which I'm about to relate right now!"

Chapter 46

Melpomone held her audience rapt, with only one or two interruptions for queries, for nearly an hour. When it was apparent that she had finished, there was a general buzz of conversation, during which there was an appeal from the principal speaker for "A cup of lapsang souchong, please, someone!" and others also turned to sipping tea and other beverages, until Norman stood up and said, "Ladies and gentlemen, I must thank Melpomene for all she has done, especially for me, as it might be said that it was I who triggered this business off. And I have some news that I would like to give now, as this seems a suitable occasion. There are two items, one of a business nature, and one domestic."

He took a sip from his glass of wine, and continued, "On my suggestion, the chairman of the board of directors of Winstanley Holdings, Sir Ansett Browne, has readily agreed to call for the resignation, *en bloc*, of the whole board, including himself. There will be a shareholders' meeting convened in six weeks' time, at which nominations for a new board will be called and then put to a general vote. Invitations and proxy documents have been sent out to all registered shareholders. In the interim, all immediate decisions affecting any of the Winstanley mills, including Gormsby's, such as the introduction of proper testing of supplied yarn quality, will be taken by Sir Ansett in collaboration with Brigadier Winter, a long-established board member who is not up for reelection."

There was applause here, even from those unaware of the extent of skulduggery that had been taking place.

Then Norman rose again, saying, "My second announcement is of a completely different nature. My dear wife, Melinda, and I are shortly to become parents! I must confess that I have been extraordinarily naïve in this matter, not attaching any significance to her recent episodes of indisposition, merely concluding she was getting a bit moody! I am terribly sorry, my dear, and I hope I can make it up to you!"

Another round of general applause, even more enthusiastic, greeted this announcement. Several ladies, including Melpomene and her Mama, embraced Melinda, who was weeping freely, but with a shy smile on her face.

Alex drew Norman aside and congratulated him on both points, saying, "At last there is a prospect of running your mill and the others on strictly ethical – albeit commercial – lines. You must be very relieved!"

"Yes, Alex, and this is largely due to the efforts of Melpomene and yourself! I believe that I am not betraying any confidences in telling you that Sir Ansett is to ask the new board to approve, as one of the first items on its agenda after it convenes, an *ex gratia* payment to Crabbe and Crabbe in consideration of services rendered! I have no idea of the amount that will be decided upon, but it I expect it will be substantial! Of course the activities of the various police forces have also been important, but as public servants they can expect no recompense save the satisfaction of jobs well done!"

Alex called Melpomene over and gave her a quick idea of what Norman had just said, to which she responded, "I am very gratified, of course, but we should not forget that there remains much unfinished business. I believe that Michael Stoddart will be arrested as soon as he can be found and will then be charged with assault and conspiracy to kidnap me. I shall have great pleasure in giving evidence before any hearing on these matters! But further, Norman, has any thought been given to ways of dealing with the erstwhile company secretary, Wilfred Hutchinson? All we have, I think, are dark suspicions – maybe we should devote our next efforts to investigating this shadowy gentleman."

The audience started to disperse; Alex and Melpomene were headed for their suite when a maid approached and said, "You are wanted on the phone, Madam, by a gentleman from the police. You can take it in the lobby annex."

It was Superintendent Wilkinson, who said, "David here, Mel – I tried your office and Marjorie told me where you were. My congratulations first on some outstanding work – for which there has been a new development. I'll first go back a little. You'll remember no doubt that one of the bodies discovered in the barn was carrying a French passport in the name of Bertrand Chausseur. I thought that as a courtesy to our colleagues across the Channel I should contact the Sûreté – I have had occasional contact with them over the years, so I asked to speak to an old acquaintance, Commissaire Principal Hugo Palance. He was very interested and told me that he was already having Chausseur investigated, as a suspect in several murders of low-level criminals. As Hugo said 'he is apparently a *décapant* – one who mops up those petty criminals who are no longer useful for the mobs!' But the interesting piece of information he had for us was that Chausseur has a sister, Antoinette Marie Françoise, who had been living with her parents in Nancy, who was rumoured to have fled to England to avoid arrest on a fraud charge and got married there!"

"Oh, ho!" said Melpomene, "So did you follow this fascinating piece of information up?" "Of course, and to cut a long story short, what you have already guessed turned out to be the case! She married Michael Stoddart about four or five years ago!"

Melpomene asked, "I hope you immediately had them arrested?" to which Wilkinson replied, "Well, I had a warrant issued but they have both gone to ground! But, following routine procedure in the case of criminals with foreign connections, I got the Met to have a watch placed on all the channel ports. We had a photograph of Stoddart taken from the last Annual Report of Winstanley Holdings, which we duplicated and sent out. So far, I must confess, there have been no sightings."

"I hope you also covered the airports," said Mel, "Stoddart has been acting as a wealthy man for a while, so he might have considered travelling by air, expensive though it may be." David exclaimed, "I overlooked that, drat it! I'll get on to it straight away and ring you back!"

Melpomene put down the phone and turned to Alec, "Do they still put the flight schedules for Croydon in the papers? Let us see." Turning to the back page of The Clarion, she read out, "Today, Croydon to Paris, Imperial Airways Flight 22. Take off time 11.30, arrives Le Bourget 2.45. They may have caught that one. The next flight to Paris is at the same time the day after tomorrow – they only fly twice a week by the look of things."

After nearly an hour, the phone rang again; it was David, "Looks as though we missed them! I had Inspector Wright ring the customs officials at Croydon, and they recorded a couple, travelling on a French passport as Monsieur and Madame Tourbillion, of Nancy, who were the right age and general appearance. All the other passengers were English businessmen travelling alone, except for one who had his 'niece' with him. Their plane is expected at Le Bourget – I alerted Hugo, and he will have them intercepted and call me back with the outcome."

Chapter 47

As Melpomene and Alex were going to their suite to bathe and dress for dinner, David Wilkinson telephoned again. Alex took the call, saying, "So, David, what news from Paris?"

"Some good and some bad!" replied Superintendent Wilkinson, "The customs people at Le Bourget have intercepted the so-called Tourbillions and given them into the custody of the French police. Commissaire Palance was informed, and he has just telephoned me, to tell me this but also to warn me that, under French law, there is a limit of 48 hours for which persons can be detained without charge. After that they must be released, and we shall lose track of them. And, in order for them to be charged they must be formally identified and their connection to a crime shown. They, of course, are claiming that they are ordinary citizens going about their legal business, and know nothing about anyone of the name of Stoddart or about any crime."

Alex passed this information to Melpomene, and then said, "How can we get over this, David? Won't the photograph you have from the annual report be convincing enough?" "Hugo Palance says not," he replied, "a single picture is not considered adequate evidence – especially as it not particularly clear. Somebody who knows Stoddart will have to go over there."

Alex thought a moment and said, "It will be difficult, David, but let me see whether I can use all my powers of persuasion to induce Melpomene to take an aeroplane trip to Paris – we know there is another flight the day after tomorrow!"

Melpomene had been listening, of course, and said, "Oh, give me the telephone, Alex, before I go completely mad! David, this is Mel. What is the deadline now – when does the 48 hours run out? I can get there on the corresponding flight in two days' time – will that be early enough?"

"As long as there are no delays!" said David, "The Stoddarts were taken into custody about two hours after their flight arrived. I will ask Hugo Palance to make arrangements for you to be met at Le Bourget and rushed to see Stoddart straight away. All you will have to do then is make a written statement saying you have identified him as the one who assaulted you and had you kidnapped, and after that we can make leisurely arrangements for him to brought back here under escort."

"That's excellent, David!" said Mel, "It will give me great satisfaction to confront this man! All I'm worried about now is whether we can get a booking on that flight!"

"Leave that to me!" said David, "If necessary, I can pull rank and have some unfortunate businessman bumped off the plane to make room for you. This is official police business! I'll ring again when arrangements have been made. Enough for now – Mrs Wilkinson is making noises in the background about burnt dinners already – the life of a policeman's wife is a hard one!"

There was no risk of spoilt dinners at Woodhampton Castle Hotel, of course, but Mel and Alex were certainly ready for their meal before they were ready to join the other guests.

Over dinner, Melpomene told her Mama and Aunt Isabel about her proposed flight to France. Aunt Isabel said, "Oh dear, I don't think you will be able to get a flying helmet and goggles here in Woodhampton – you will probably have to go up to the Army and Navy Stores in London or somewhere like that!"

Mel smiled and gently explained that air liners nowadays had enclosed cabins, with heating and everything! "The one I shall travel on is called a de Havilland Hercules, and it has a cabin for six or seven passengers, sitting in comfortable chairs! If you like, you can come to Croydon and see me take off!"

"Oh, no dear, thanks all the same! I should be far too nervous! How will the pilot find his way to Paris?" Several diners were only too keen to explain everything to the old lady – some of them had seen airliners taking off and landing, but nobody there had actually flown!

The next day, Melpomene persuaded Alex, with hardly any difficulty, to play a vigorous game of tennis with her, saying, "We've had plenty of excitement recently, but not much exercise! I particularly need to loosen up, after that long drive pretending to be unconscious – you'd be surprised, Alex, how difficult that was!"

And in the afternoon, Alex remembered the case notes that Marjorie had given them as they left the office. He found the folder, which they had carefully put away in a drawer, and opened it up. The first item was a catalogue for an art exhibition, which he flicked through before setting it aside.

Then came a transcript of notes of a conversation Marjorie had conducted with the client, which started, '*Notes on a request by Mr Alastair DuPlessis: Mr DuPlessis is an expensively-dressed gentleman, probably in his middle forties, with abundant hair, greying at the temples, of middle height and a trifle portly.*'

Alex grunted appreciatively, "Marjorie is certainly a treasure – she understands the need to record one's initial impressions! I'll read on ..."

'*He owns a long-established art dealership in Kensington, and explained that he had approached Crabbe and Crabbe, rather than going to the police in the first instance, because he wished to be meticulous in avoiding accusations. His clientele included a wide variety of reputable art dealers and gallery owners, and we would appreciate that commercial reputation in this area is a fragile commodity. To get swiftly to the point, he said that a valued customer had discovered that a painting he had sold him, as an eighteenth-century work by a famous painter – he would give us full details later – was, the customer claimed, a clear forgery. Could we please investigate, with the utmost discretion. The work in question is pictured on page 14 of the enclosed catalogue, with the title "Daphnis and Chloe with Putti".*'

"This would certainly make a change from our recent work, Mel – what do you say? Should we take it on? It will require extensive background research, I would think."

Melpomene pondered for a few seconds, then said, "Let's go for it Alex! No fees were discussed by Marjorie, as was proper, but he sounds as though he could stand our rates – however we set them! Ring Marjorie and ask her to give him a holding reply, on the understanding it will be a few days until we are free to start. If he is serious he will take this as a responsible course of action on our part."

Alex telephoned the office and told Marjorie all this. She said that DuPlessis had rung up and asked that morning what was happening, and she had said she would let him know as soon as she could, so this was timely. If he had problems she would tell Alex about them. Alex explained that Melpomene would be out of reach for a while, "As she will be buzzing about the stratosphere between here and France on other business – we'll let you know how that comes out as soon as it is resolved, of course."

"Half her luck!" said Marjorie.

Chapter 48

After looking through the DuPlessis notes again, Alex asked Mel if she wanted to play some more tennis, but she said, "Enough is enough, my dear! This afternoon I intend to take things more quietly – after all, tomorrow is likely to be full of excitement, one way and another. No, I think I might do a crossword or two and finish off my Ethel M Dell book – even though its dénouement is becoming only too obvious! What will you do, Alex?"

"First, I'll ring David Wilkinson and make sure everything is set for your excursion tomorrow, and then I'll call Wally Simmonds in Huddersfield to see whether there have been any more developments in his enquiries about Hutchinson. And I'll ask him, as a matter of courtesy, to pass on the latest developments to Dr Bullock and Tessa McPherson."

After an hour, Alex popped his head back into their sitting room, where he found Mel with her feet up, a tea-tray strategically placed by her side. "Ethel was as predictable as I thought!" she said, "So I'm on today's Times crossword after knocking off yesterday's. What news from the Rialto?"

"Your flight is all fixed!" said Alex, "We'll meet David in the main hall at Croydon, and he will give you the tickets – he's booked a return flight for you for the next day, not knowing how long the Stoddart business will take – and he has a sworn warrant for Stoddart's arrest for you to pass to the French police, as well as a letter of introduction to Commissaire Principal Palance. Don't forget your passport!"

"Splendid!" said Mel, "And did you speak to Simmonds?"

"Yes, I did. He tells me that he sent one of his detective-sergeants to Hutchinson's home, where his wife told him that he was 'away on business.' She didn't know – or wouldn't say – where, so the sergeant went next to Hutchinson's office in the city – he is a solicitor in a small way of business as well as acting as Company Secretary for Winstanley – and the girl there confirmed that he was 'away on business' at some unknown place. She added that she 'sometimes doesn't see him for weeks at a time.' So, the quest continues. I told Wally Simmonds all about Stoddart's flight to France and your expedition to seize him, and he was mightily amused, saying 'If I had Daphne – I mean Melpomene – pursuing me, I would be shivering in my boots! I hope she's not packing a Luger this time!' I asked him to brief Bullock and Tessa, too."

"No, Alex, I shall certainly not be taking your Luger – you probably need some special sort of licence to take out of the country, and anyway I imagine the French authorities would jib at a private citizen bringing a fire-arm into their country. It sounds as though I'm developing some sort of reputation in the police force, and maybe in criminal circles too, as a pistol-wielding avenger! I shall not be too quick to deny this – it might be useful on occasions!"

They arrived at Croydon airport in plenty of time, and had coffee with David Wilkinson as he handed Mel the tickets and all the papers, which she stowed in the small overnight bag she was carrying over her shoulder. "You will be met at le Bourget by an Inspecteur Sylvestre, who will then take you to meet Hugo Palance at the Sûreté in Paris, where the Stoddarts are being held. Hugo is fully briefed, of course. I shall be on tenterhooks until this is all resolved, I must admit!"

Soon a stewardess arrived to take Mel to the plane. The others walked with her to the doors which gave onto the field, where her passport was checked, and stood waving as she was led to the airliner – a huge biplane with three engines, propellers already turning, and a fuselage as long as a bus. Melpomene turned and waved as she went up two or three steps to the cabin door, holding her hat on against the wind from the propellers. As soon as she was inside, ground staff secured the door, signalled the pilot in his cockpit above the cabin, and removed the chocks in front of the wheels. With a loud roar from the engines, the plane turned in a large semicircle and started to speed across the grass. After a couple of hundred yards, the watchers saw it lift off the ground and climb steadily until it was out of sight.

Inside the cabin, Melpomene found that there were only four other passengers as well as the stewardess, so she had a choice of seats, which were all next to the windows. She sat down and saw that they were climbing steadily. By craning she could see the patchwork of fields, with an occasional village or farmhouse slipping away – a fascinating sight for a passenger making a first flight. But at least two of her fellow passengers were blasé enough that they were reading the newspaper or studying files from their briefcases.

The stewardess came round with a couple of thermos flasks, asking, "Tea or coffee, madam, or I think I have orange juice?" Melpomene politely declined, not knowing whether or not this class of airliner had lavatory facilities!

It wasn't long before she could see, through breaks in the fluffy white clouds, that they were over the sea, and Mel found she was slightly relieved when land came in sight once more!

But it was not long before the stewardess announced that the plane would soon be landing, and that passengers should keep seated and hold on to the sides of their seats, as there might be a jolt as the wheels touched down.

Safely inside the airport building, Mel was approached by a man in police uniform who smiled and tipped his cap, saying "Madame Crabbe, n'est-ce pas? I am Sylvestre, at your service."

He led her out of the hall, waving away the customs official, and took her to a low black car, with the driver saluting and holding the door open for her, while Sylvestre got in at the other side. As they set off, he said, "If Madame is interested in automobiles, this is our new standard police car, which has been introduced only this year, a Citroën 'Traction Avant', called like that because, unusually, the engine drives the front wheels."

Melpomene decided to reward his obvious enthusiasm, "We have an Alvis roadster at home, which I love dearly!" to which her companion kissed his fingers, saying "Ah, c'est une auto très très belle, aussi!"

The trip to Sûreté headquarters was a touch hair-raising, the driver being apparently as enthusiastic about the car as Inspecteur Sylvestre, but they made it in one piece, and Mel was taken to Hugo Palance's impressive office and introduced to the Commissaire Principal.

He kissed her hand and said, "Very happy to meet you, Madame. And David Wilkinson, he is well I hope? Can I offer you a cup of coffee or perhaps a tisane? No? Later, perhaps. And I should mention that I hope you will do my wife and I the honour of having dinner in our home, and spending the night with us there? David tells me you will return to England tomorrow."

"But now to business. You have the arrest warrant? Wonderful! I will take you to confront this reprobate immediately!"

Chapter 49

Melpomene went with Hugo Palance and a secretary carrying a note-pad to an interview room, divided by a counter and a wire-mesh screen – to discourage physical assaults, she supposed. They seated themselves and then Michael Stoddart was led in the other side by a uniformed policeman.

He was looking even more grey and ill than the last time she had seen him, and staggered a little as he was pushed toward a seat. Commissaire Palance said, "This interview will be conducted in the English language. Are you Michael Graham Stoddart, also known as Michel Tourbillion?"

"Yes, sir, my name as recorded on the official English Register of Births, Marriages and Deaths, is Michael Graham Stoddart."

"I shall hereafter address you as Stoddart," said Palance, "You have been brought here to answer to an official warrant of arrest duly issued by a magistrate in England, that I have with me here, in which you are accused of assault, deprivation of liberty and kidnap of this lady here present, the Honourable Melpomene Henrietta Crabbe, née Musgrave, of 24 Archer Street, in the city and county of London. Madame Crabbe, do you identify this man as the perpetrator of these offences?"

"I certainly do!" said Melpomene, "And I still have bruises on my arm that he inflicted while he was rendering me unconscious by administering chloroform!"

"That is all that we require at this stage, thank you, Madame Crabbe – you will be able to go into detail when Stoddart is tried. By the rights conferred on me by the President, the Chamber of Deputies and the Senate of the Republic of France, I hereby order that Stoddart be handed over to the English authorities as soon as possible, so that he may be tried in an appropriate court in England. Take the prisoner Stoddart away!"

When Stoddart had been taken from the room, Palance and Melpomene shook hands warmly. Then Mel asked, "What will happen with Antoinette Stoddart?"

"Well, by whatever name, she is claimed by the French judicial system, to face charges of fraud dating back half a dozen years! The reason that we haven't arrested her before is that she was

145

in England, and fraud is not covered by the extradition treaties between France and England. Now, I think we both deserve some refreshment!"

Commissaire Palance took Mel back to his office where they had coffee and the promised tisane and chatted about their current cases of interest, Hugo Palance describing how Sûreté agents were engaged in the final stages of gathering up the conspirators in an extensive smuggling operation involving European and North African countries.

Then Melpomene was taken on a rapid tour of the headquarters building before being shown to the Commissaire's official car, not a 'Traction' this time but a dignified DeLage limousine, which Hugo explained proudly was the same model favoured by the King of Siam and other Eastern potentates.

At the Palance residence, Mel was welcomed warmly by Madame Palance, "Call me Louise, please! My name is really Huguette, but that is much too close to my husband's name, so that together we could be taken for a music-hall act!"

The evening was spent very pleasantly over a delicious dinner, followed by a selection of art songs sung by Louise in a rich contralto, accompanied by Hugo at the piano. Melpomene declined to sing!

The next morning the Palance chauffeur took Mel to the airport, unaccompanied by Hugo who said that he was devastated but felt that he had unfortunately to attend to matters of duty rather than pleasure.

The airliner this time was not a de Havilland, but a smaller French Breguet single-engine biplane, with a cabin for six. Nevertheless the flight was just as comfortable as before, and Mel was soon at Croydon being welcomed by Alex and David Wilkinson.

Uncharacteristically, David gave Melpomene a hug, showing how happy he was, "Wheels are now in motion, and Mr Stoddart will soon receive his just deserts! And by the way, we found that one of your two victims, Mel, now languishing in hospital due to your accurate shooting, fired the fatal shots at the men in the barn – the Luger and the bullets matched perfectly. It should not be too difficult to show that his companion was an accomplice and so equally guilty of those

146

murders, to say nothing of their part in your abduction, my dear!"

The three made a modest celebration of tea and cakes in the airport café, and then parted, David in his police car to Scotland Yard to deliver the case documents, and Alex and Melpomene – driving the Alvis, of course – back to the Woodhampton Castle Hotel, mainly to tell Mel's Mama and her aunts all about her aerial adventures.

As they drove, they chatted, mainly wondering how many more loose ends there still remained, "To tell you the truth," said Melpomene, "I am not too concerned at this stage. We have achieved a great deal, and I'm sure Hutchinson will eventually get his come-uppance without any further work from Crabbe and Crabbe – what do you say, partner?"

"I agree, Mel – it looks as though Gormsby's and the other mills in the group will go on from strength to strength now. I wonder what will happen to the Pilkington empire though – department stores, mansions, factories, the lot? I suppose sorting out all the rival claims will be a matter for the courts. Happily we don't intend to get involved in that sort of litigation ourselves, do we?"

"Not unless we get asked, Alex!"

That evening in the hotel, they found they were the guests of honour at a grand celebratory dinner. Some of the guests were local and therefore not surprising, but a contingent from Huddersfield – Tessa McPherson, Kenneth Bullock and Walter Simmonds, as well as Ansett and Felicity Browne – and from London – Jimmy Manley and DC Thompson, who blushingly admitted his first name was Cecil, who had been suggested by David Wilkinson to the hostess, Lady Cynthia.

All in all it was a delightful evening, even though small knots of those with common interests – such as police detectives – had to be broken up and persuaded to mix. This was helped when Stephen Buckmaster sat at the piano, played a couple of solo pieces and then appealed to the gathering to put aside their modesty and join him in whatever ways they could, revealing that Lady Cynthia was a passable lyric soprano, that Jimmy Manley had a talent for Cockney comedy recitations and that Tessa McPherson travelled nowhere without her Gaelic harp – whose sweet tone gave a wonderful accompaniment to her folksongs! All in all, everyone had a good time!

147

Chapter 50

After breakfast, Melpomene and Alex were loading up their Alvis, and going the rounds and saying goodbye to everyone, when Alex was called to the phone once again.

It was David Wilkinson, reporting, "Michael Stoddart is in the Croydon General Hospital, under guard, but receiving intensive care while undergoing a series of tests. He collapsed as he was being led off the RAF aeroplane that was sent to pick him up from Le Bourget. I had a preliminary report from the emergency room doctor, who says that he appears to be suffering from some internal disorder, but that more tests are needed and are being conducted right now."

"My word!" said Alex, "Melpomene told us he was looking very ill in Paris – and we noticed before that he was looking pretty shaky when we saw him at Fenster and Churchman's spinning mill in Leeds."

He told Melpomene all this, and she said, "Yes, but I've always wondered whether it had anything to do with the shock he seemed to get from the telephone call when we were at the Browne's that evening. He looked pretty bad then and had to go home. What could it have been? Let me talk to David."

"Its Mel, David," she said, "tell me what you think of this. I only just thought of it, so maybe it's crazy. I reckon that the doctor looking after him should ask him straight out if he can say what happened at Sir Ansett's house that night, because that's where it seems to have all started. He could point out that he has nothing to lose by telling, and everything to gain if he wants to get well again. What do you say?"

"It's certainly worth a try, Mel – I'll put it to Doctor Williams when I get his progress report on the tests. I'll let you know as soon as I find out anything. Will you still be there later, or are you going back to London?"

"Yes, we are going soon, give us a call on our office number, David, we should be there after about two o'clock."

They had a good run home, stopping half way only briefly for the statutory cup of tea, and reached the office before two.

Marjorie was glad to see them, and said that she had set up a preliminary appointment with Mr DuPlessis, the gallery owner, for 1 pm on the following Monday, "Is that all right? I can change it if it isn't – Mr DuPlessis seems a very reasonable genleman. And there was a telephone call for Alex a few minutes ago from a Dr Williams at Croydon General Hospital – he left his direct number for you. He sounded quite excited!"

Alex rang the number, while Melpomene took the second earpiece, "Alex Crabbe here – you have some results for Mr Stoddart I believe." "Yes, Mr Crabbe, I certainly do, Superintendent Wilkinson suggested I speak directly to you – this patient is suffering from a severe case of mercury poisoning! Fortunately, once diagnosed, the treatment for this is straightforward, though it may take some time before he is completely fit again. I have insisted to the police that he be left in my care, under guard if necessary, until I'm satisfied, before he is taken, as I understand, to prison."

"Thank you Doctor! Have you any idea at the moment how the mercury was administered?"

"No, I have not been able to question him at length yet, but I did notice something that might be a clue – his mouth is stained a deep red, which suggests to me that he might have ingested Mercurochrome, a commonly-used antiseptic – you may remember having it applied to your skinned knees when you were a boy!"

"Thank you again Doctor, I will keep in touch for further developments."

"Very interesting indeed!" said Melpomene, "I shall now telephone Felicity Browne in Huddersfield! Can you get me her number, Marjorie, please?"

When the call was answered, Mel took over, "Good afternoon, Felicity, it was so nice that you and Ansett came to dinner with us yesterday! Now I have what may seem at first to be a couple of strange questions for you. First, in your house, is there a bathroom or lavatory close to the room where you keep your telephone? Second, do you keep your first-aid materials there – bandages, ointments and the like? If so, please go in there and tell me whether you have, on the one hand, mouthwash, and on the other, Mercurochrome, that red stuff you put on sores and cuts? Please pop and see, and tell me what you find, please."

There was a short pause and then Melpomene responded to Felicity's answer, "You do? Do the two bottles look alike at all? – Wonderful! Now we can have a good guess what happened to dear Mr Stoddart – he glugged a bottle of Mercurochrome by mistake for mouthwash! He was probably upset by a call from the delightful Mr Pilkington – likely a dire threat, knowing that gentleman's style – and got himself all fussed up! That's my working hypothesis for the moment, anyway. When he is lucid again, he can tell us himself! Thank you again, Felicity!"

Melpomene turned away from the telephone, beaming, "I declare the case of the trouble at the mill well and truly wrapped up – as good as, anyway! Now let's have cups of tea and some of Mrs Jenkins' estimable jam tarts!"

"Now that case has been officially closed, my dear," said Alex, "we should get our minds into gear for Mr DuPlessis. Should we have a trip to the Victoria and Albert and look through the relevant galleries? Or there may be useful books in the University College library, perhaps."

"Let's not get ahead of ourselves, Alex, we might risk cluttering our poor old brains up with all sorts of irrelevancies. Let us see what the client himself has to say. My chief concern is deciding on an outfit that will appear professional without being drear, nor looking as though I have come straight from Ascot!"

"Nor even from the chorus line at the Windmill! I have implicit faith in your taste, Melpomene. I myself will wear a velvet beret and a smock, with a silk scarf carelessly tied around my neck. And sandals, of course!"

"And I suggest we all go to the pictures tonight, to celebrate and wind down," said Melpomene, "I believe they are showing 'The Son of the Sheik' with Vilma Banky and Rudolph Valentino at the Odeon – are you coming, Marjorie?"

"Yes, that would be lovely, but let's have dinner first, can we. I've been bringing sandwiches to work the last few days!"

"Will our usual Italian place suit you, then?" "Oh, yes please!"

FIN

KEEP VIGILANT FOR THE NEXT CASE!

Crabbe and Crabbe's next case will be coming out soon!

Will there be murders? Who knows.

Will there be skullduggery? Undoubtedly.

Will Melpomene and Alex solve the case?

Of course – how could anyone doubt this!

Look out for:

"But is it Art?"

A Case for Crabbe and Crabbe.

By Geoffrey Foster

Coming later this year.

www.ingramcontent.com/pod-product-compliance
Lightning Source LLC
Chambersburg PA
CBHW052143170626
46812CB00004B/1561